pact
h the
appearance of his early novella *The Lovers*. Since then Mr Farmer's work has been noted for its open-minded thought, its humane compassion and its superb craftsmanship. With such stories as the *Carmody* and *Riverworld* series, with such extraordinary novels as *Flesh*, with his Hugo Award-winning short novel *Riders of the Purple Wage* and with the series *The World of the Tiers*, Philip José Farmer has shown a talent of the very first rank in science fiction and fantasy.

Mr Farmer was born in Peoria, Illinois, lived for many years in Los Angeles, and has recently returned with his wife to Illinois.

Also by Philip José Farmer in Sphere Books

THE ALLEY GOD
THE MAKER OF UNIVERSES
THE GATES OF CREATION
A PRIVATE COSMOS
THE GREEN ODYSSEY

Behind the Walls of Terra

PHILIP JOSÉ FARMER

SPHERE BOOKS LIMITED
30/32 Gray's Inn Road, London WC1X 8JL

First published in Great Britain by Sphere Books
Ltd 1975
Reprinted 1978

This adventure of Kickaha is dedicated to
Jack Cordes, who lives in the pocket universes
of Peoria and Pekin.

Set in Intertype Times

Printed in Great Britain by
C. Nicholls & Company Ltd
The Philips Park Press, Manchester

THE sky had been green for twenty-four years. Suddenly, it was blue.

Kickaha blinked. He was home again. Rather, he was once more on the planet of his birth. He had lived on Earth for twenty-eight years. Then he had lived for twenty-four years in that pocket universe he called The World of Tiers. Now, though he did not care to be here, he was back 'home'.

He was standing in the shadow of an enormous overhang of rock. The stone floor was swept clean by the wind that travelled along the face of the cliff. Outside the semi-cavern were mountains covered with pine and fir trees. The air was cool but would get warmer, since this was morning of a July day in southern California. Or it should be, if his calculations were correct.

Since he was high on the face of a mountain, he could see very far into the southwest. There was a great valley beyond the nearer smaller valleys, a valley which he supposed was one near the Los Angeles area. It surprised and unnerved him, because it was not at all what he had expected. It was covered with a thick gray poisonous-looking cloud, that gave the impression of being composed of many many thousands of fumes, as if the floor of the valley below the cloud were jammed with geysers boiling and bubbling and pouring out the noxious gases of internal Earth.

He had no idea of what had occurred on Earth since that night in 1946 when he had been transmitted accidentally from this universe to that of Jadawin. Perhaps the great basins of the Los Angeles area were filled with poison gas that some enemy nation had dropped. He could not guess what enemy could do this, since both Germany and Japan had been wrecked and utterly defeated when he left this world, and Russia was sorely wounded.

He shrugged. He would find out in time. The memory banks below the great fortress-palace at the top of the only planet in the universe of the green sky had said that this 'gate' opened into a place in the mountains near a lake called Arrowhead.

The gate was a circle of indestructible metal buried a few inches below the rock of the floor. Only a dimly stained ring of purple on the stone marked its presence.

Kickaha (born Paul Janus Finnegan) was six feet one inch in height, weighed one hundred and ninety pounds, and was broad-shouldered, lean-waisted, and massively thighed. His hair was red-bronze, his eyebrows were thick, dark, and arching, his eyes were leaf-green, his nose was straight but short, his upper lip was long, and his chin was deeply cleft. He wore hiking clothes and a bag on his back. In one hand he held the handle of a dark leather case which looked as if it contained a musical instrument, perhaps a horn or trumpet.

His hair was shoulder-length. He had considered cutting it before he returned to Earth, so he would not look strange. But the time had been short, and he had decided to wait until he got to a barber shop. His cover story would be that he and Anana had been in the mountains so long he had not had a chance to clip his hair.

The woman beside him was as beautiful as it was possible for a woman to be. She had long dark wavy hair, a flawless white skin, dark-blue eyes, and a superb figure. She wore hiking garb: boots, levis, a lumberman's checked shirt, and a cap with a long bill. She also carried a pack on her back in which were shoes, a dress, undergarments, a small handbag, and several devices which would have startled or shocked an Earth scientist. Her hair was done in the style of 1946, as Kickaha remembered it. She wore no make-up nor needed it. Thousands of years ago, she had permanently reddened her lips, as every female Lord had done.

He kissed the woman on the lips and said, 'You've been in a number of worlds, Anana, but I'll bet in none more weird than Earth's.'

'I've seen blue skies before,' she said. 'Wolff and Chryseis have a five-hour start on us. The Beller has a two-hour start. And all have a big world in which to get lost.'

He nodded and said, 'There was no reason for Wolff and Chryseis to hang around here, since the gate is one-way. They'll take off for the nearest two-way gate, which is in the Los Angeles area, if the gate still exists. If it doesn't, then the closest ones will be in Kentucky or Hawaii. So we know where they should be going.'

He paused and wet his lips and then said, 'As for the Beller, who knows? He could have gone anywhere or he may still be around here. He's in an absolutely strange world, he doesn't know anything about Earth, and he can't speak any of the languages.'

'We don't know what he looks like, but we'll find him. I know the Bellers,' she said. 'This one won't cache his bell and then run away to hide with the idea he'll come back later for it. A Beller cannot endure the idea of being very far away from his bell. He'll carry it around as long as he can. And that will be our only means of identifying him.'

'I know,' Kickaha said. He was having trouble breathing, and his eyes were beginning to swim. Suddenly, he was weeping.

Anana was alarmed for a minute, and then she said, 'Cry! I did it when I went back to my home world once. I thought I was dry forever, that tears were for mortals. But coming back home after so long exposed my weakness.'

Kickaha dried his tears and took his canteen from his belt, uncapped it and drank deeply.

'I love my world, the green-skied world,' he said 'I don't like Earth; I don't remember it with much affection. But I guess I had more love for it than I thought. I'll admit that, every once in a while, I had some nostalgia, some faint longing to see it again, see the people I knew. But . . .'

Below them, perhaps a thousand feet down, a two-lane macadam road curved around the side of the mountain and continued upward until it was lost around the other side. A car appeared on the upgrade, sped below them, and then was lost with the road. Kickaha's eyes widened, and he said, 'I never saw a car like that before. It looked like a little bug. A beetle!'

A hawk swung into view and, riding the currents, passed before them not more than a hundred yards.

Kichaha was delighted. 'The first red-tail I've seen since I left Indiana!'

He stepped out onto the edge, forgetting for a second, but a second only, his caution. Then he jumped back in under the protection of the overhang. He motioned to Anana, and she went to one end of the ledge and looked out while he did so at the other.

There was nobody below, as far as he could see, though the many trees could conceal anybody who did not want to be seen. He went out a little further and looked upward then but could not see past the overhang. The way down was not apparent at first, but investigation revealed projections just below the right side of the ledge. These would have to do for a start, and, once they began climbing down, other hand and footholds had to appear.

Kickaha eased himself backward over the ledge, feeling with his foot for a projection. Then he pulled himself back up and lay down on the edge and again scrutinized the road and the forest a thousand feet below. A number of blue-jays had started screaming somewhere below him; the air acted as a funnel to siphon the faint cries to him.

He took a pair of small binoculars from his shirt pocket and adjusted three dials on their surface. Then he removed an ear phone and a thin wire with a male jack on one end and plugged the jack into the receptacle on the side of the binoculars. He began to sweep the forest below and eventually centred it on that spot where the jays were raising such a ruckus.

Through the device, the distant forest suddenly became close, and the faint noises were loud. Something dark moved, and, after he readjusted the binoculars, he saw the face of a man. More sweepings of the device and more adjusting enabled him to see parts of three other men. Each was armed with a rifle with scope, and two had binoculars.

Kickaha gave the device to Anana so she could see for herself. He said, 'As far as you know, Red Orc is the only Lord on Earth?'

She put the glasses down and said, 'Yes.'

'He must know about these gates, then, and he's set up some sort of alarm device, so he knows when they're activated. Maybe his men are stationed close, maybe far off. Maybe Wolff and Chryseis and the Beller got away before his men could get here. Maybe not. In any case, they're waiting for us.'

They did not comment about the lack of a permanent trap at the gates or a permanent guard. Red Orc, or whatever Lord was responsible for these men, would make a game out of the invasion of his home territory by other Lords. It was deadly but nevertheless a game.

Kickaha went back to viewing the four beneath the trees. Presently, he said. 'They've got a walkie-talkie.'

He heard a whirring sound above him. He rolled over to look up and saw a strange machine that had just flown down over the mountain to his right.

He said, 'An autogyro!' and then the machine was hidden by a spur of the mountain. He jumped up and ran into the cavern with Anana behind him.

The chopping sound of a plane's rotors became a roar and then the machine was hovering before the ledge. Kickaha became aware that the machine was not a true autogyro. As far as he knew, a gyro could not stand still in the air, or, as this was doing, swing from side to side or turn around one spot.

The body of the craft was transparent; he could see the pilot and three men inside, armed with rifles. He and Anana were trapped; they had no place to run or hide.

Undoubtedly, Orc's men had been sent to find out what weapons the intruders carried. Under these conditions, the intruders would have to use their weapons, unless they preferred to be captured. They did not so prefer. They spoke the activating code word, aimed the rings at the machine, and spoke the final word.

The needle-thin golden rays spat once, delivering the full charges in the rings' tiny powerpacks.

The fuselage split in two places, and the plane fell. Kickaha ran out and looked down over the ledge in time to see the pieces strike the side of the mountain below. One section went up in a white and red ball which fissioned into a dozen smaller fire globes. All the pieces eventually fell not too far apart near the bottom and burned fiercely.

The four men under the trees were white-faced, and the man with the walkie-talkie spat words into the transmitter. Kickaha tried to tighten the beam so he could pick them up, but the noise from the burning machine interfered.

Kickaha was glad that he had struck the first blow, but his elation was darkened. He knew that the Lord had deliberately sacrificed the men in the gyro in order to find out how dangerous his opponents were. Kickaha would have preferred to have gotten away undetected. Moreover, getting down the mountainside would be impossible until night fell. In the meantime, the Lord would attack again.

He and Anana recharged their rings with the tiny powerpacks. He kept a watch on the men below while she scanned the sides of the mountain. Presently, a red convertible appeared on the left, going down the mountain road. A man and a woman sat in it. The car stopped near the flaming wreckage and the two got out to investigate. They stood around talking and then they got back into the car and sped off.

Kickaha grinned. No doubt they were going to notify the authorities. That meant that the four men would be powerless to attack. On the other hand, the authorities might climb up here and find him and Anana. He could claim that they were just hikers, and the authorities could not hold them for long. But just to be in custody for a while would enable the Lord to seize them the moment they were released. Also, he and Anana would have a hard time identifying themselves, and it was possible that the authorities might hold them until they could be identified.

They would have no record of Anana, of course, but if they tracked down his fingerprints, they would find something difficult to explain. They would discover that he was Paul Janus Finnegan, born in 1918 near Terre Haute, Indiana, that he had served in a tank corps of the Eighth Army during World War II, and that he had mysteriously disappeared in 1946 from his apartment in a building in Bloomington while he was attending the University of Indiana, and that he had not been seen since.

He could always claim amnesia, of course, but how would he explain that he was fifty-two years old chronologically yet only twenty-five years old physiologically? And how would he explain the origin of the peculiar devices in his backpack?

He cursed softly in Tishquetmoac, in Half-Horse Lakotah, in the Middle High German of Dracheland, in the language of the Lords, and in English. And then he switched his thinking into English, because he had half-forgotten that language and had to get accustomed to its use. If those four men stuck there until the authorities showed up . . .

But the four were not staying. After a long conversation, and obvious receipt of orders from the walkie-talkie, they left. They climbed up onto the road, and within a minute a car appeared from the right. It stopped, and the four got in and drove off.

Kickaha considered that this might be a feint to get him and Anana to climb down the mountain. Then another gyro would catch them on the mountainside, or the men would come back. Or both.

But if he waited until the police showed up, he could not come down until nightfall. Orc's men would be waiting down there, and they might have some of the Lords' advanced weapons to use, because they would not fear to use them at night and in this remote area.

'Come on,' he said to Anana in English. 'We're going down now. If the police see us, we'll tell them we're just hitchhikers. You leave the talking to me; I'll tell them you're Finnish and don't speak English yet. Let's hope there'll be no Finns among them.'

'What?' Anana said. She had spent three and a half

years on Earth in the 1880s and had learned some English and more French but had forgotten the little she had known.

Kickaha repeated slowly.

'It's your world,' she said in English. 'You're the boss.'

He grinned at that, because very few female Lords ever admitted that there was any situation in which the male was their master. He let himself down again over the ledge. He was beginning to sweat. The sun was coming over the mountain now and shining fully on them, but this did not account for his perspiration. He was sweating out the possible reappearance of the Lord's men.

He and Anana had gotten about one-third of the way down when the first police car appeared. It was black and white and had a big star on the side. Two men got out. Their uniforms looked like those of state police, as he remembere those of the Midwest.

A few minutes later, another patrol car and an ambulance appeared. Then two more cars stopped. After a while, there were ten cars.

Kickaha found a path that was sometimes precarious but led at an angle to the right along the slope. He and Anana could keep hidden from the people below part of the time. If they should be seen, they would not have to stop. The police could come after them, but they would be so far behind that their pursuit would be hopeless.

Or so it seemed until another gyro appeared. This one swept back and forth, apparently looking for bodies or survivors. Kickaha and Anana hid behind a large boulder until the craft landed near the road. Then they continued their sidewise descent of the mountain.

When they reached the road, they drank some water and ate some of the concentrated food they had brought from the other world. Kickaha told her that they would walk along the road, going downward. He also reminded her that Red Orc's men would be cruising up and down the road looking for them.

'Then why don't we hide out until nightfall?' she said.

'Because in the daylight I can spot a car that definitely won't be Orc's. I won't mind being picked up by one of them. But if Orc's men show up and try anything, we have our rays and we can be on guard. At night, you won't know who's stopping to pick you up. We could avoid the road altogether and hike alongside it in the woods, but that's slow going. I don't want Wolff or the Beller to get too far ahead.'

'How do we know they didn't both go the other way?' she said. 'Or that Red Orc didn't pick them up?'

'We don't,' he said. 'But I'm betting that this is the way to Los Angeles. It's westward, and it's downhill. Wolff would know this, and the instinct of the Beller would be to go down, I would think. I could be wrong. But I can't stand here forever trying to make up my mind what happened. Let's go.'

They started off. The air was sweet and clean; birds sang; a squirrel ran out onto the branch of a tall and half-dead pine and watched them with its bright eyes. There were a number of dead or dying pines. Evidently, some plant disease had struck them. The only signs of human beings were the skeletal power transmission towers and aluminium cables going up the side of a mountain. Kickaha explained to Anana what they were; he was going to be doing much explaining from now on. He did not mind. It gave her the opportunity to learn English and him the opportunity to relearn it.

A car passed them from behind. On hearing it, Kickaha and Anana withdrew from the side of the road, ready to shoot their ray rings or to leap down the slope of the mountain if they had to. He gestured with his thumb at the car, which held a man, woman, and two children. The car did not even slow down. Then a big truck pulling a trailer passed them. The driver looked as if he might be going to stop but he kept on going.

Anana said, 'These vehicles! So primitive! So noisy! And they stink!'

'Yes, but we *do* have atomic power,' Kickaha said. 'At

least, we had atomic bombs. America did anyway. I thought that by now they'd have atomic-powered cars. They've had a whole generation to develop them.'

A cream-coloured station wagon with a man and woman and two teenagers passed them. Kickaha stared after the boy. He had hair as long as Kickaha's and considerably less disciplined. The girl had long yellow hair that fell smoothly over her shoulders, and her face was thickly made-up. Like a whore's, he thought. Were those really green eyelids?

The parents, who looked about fifty, seemed normal. Except that she had a hairdo that was definitely not around in 1946. And her make-up had been heavy, too, although not nearly as thick as the girl's.

None of the cars that he had seen were identifiable. Some of them had a GM emblem, but that was the only familiar thing. This was to be expected, of course. But he was startled when the next car to pass was the beetle he had seen when he first looked down from the ledge. Or at least it looked enough like it to be the same. VW? What did that stand for?

He had expected many changes, some of which would not be easy to understand. He could think of no reason why such an ugly cramped car as the VW would be accepted, although he did remember the little Willys of his adolescence. He shrugged. It would take too much energy and time to figure out the reasons for everything he saw. If he were to survive, he would have to concentrate on the immediate problem: getting away from Red Orc's men. If they were Red Orc's.

He and Anana walked swiftly in a loose-jointed gait. She was beginning to relax and to take an interest in the beauty of their surroundings. She smiled and squeezed his hand once and said, 'I love you.'

He kissed her on the cheek and said, 'I love you, too.'

She was beginning to sound and act like an Earthwoman, instead of the superaristocratic Lord.

He heard a car coming around the bend a quarter of a mile away and glanced back at it. It was a black and white state police car with two golden-helmeted men. He looked straight ahead but out of the side of his mouth said, 'If this car stops, act easy. It's the police. Let me handle things. If I hold up two fingers, run and jump down the side of the mountain. No! On second thought ... listen, we'll go with them. They can take us into town, or near it, and then we'll stun them with the rings. Got it?'

The car, however, shot by without even scowling.

Kickaha breathed relief and said, 'We don't look as suspicious as I feel.'

They walked on down the road. As they came onto a half-mile stretch, they heard a faint roar behind them. The sound became louder, and then Kickaha grinned with pleasure. 'Motorcycles,' he said. 'Lots of them.'

The roaring became very loud. They turned, and saw about twenty big black cycles race like a black cloud around the corner of the mountain. Kickaha was amazed. He had never seen men or women dressed like these. Several of them aroused a reflex he had thought dead since peace was declared in 1945. His hand flew to the handle of the knife in his belt sheath, and he looked for a ditch into which to dive.

Three of the cyclists wore German coalscuttle helmets with big black swastikas painted on the grey metal. They also wore Iron Crosses or metal swastikas on chains around their necks.

All wore dark glasses, and these, coupled with the men's beards or handlebar moustaches and sideburns, and the women's heavy make-up, made their faces seem insectile. Their clothing was dark, although a few men wore dirty once-white T-shirts. Most wore calf-length boots. A woman sported a kepi and a dragoon's bright-red, yellow-piped jacket. Their black leather jackets and T-shirts bore skulls and crossbones that looked like phalluses, and the legend: LUCIFER'S LOUTS.

The cavalcade went roaring by, some gunning their motors or waving at the two and several wove back and forth across the road, leaning far over to both sides with their arms folded. Kickaha grinned appreciatively at that; he had owned and loved a motorcycle when he was going to high school in Terre Haute.

Anana, however, wrinkled up her nose. 'The stink of fuel is bad enough,' she said. 'But did you smell *them*? They haven't bathed for weeks. Or months.'

'The Lord of this world has been very lax,' Kickaha said.

He referred to the sanitary habits of the human inhabitants of the pocket universes which the other Lords ruled. Although the Lords were often very cruel with their human property, they insisted on cleanliness and beauty. They had established laws and religious precepts which saw to it that cleanliness was part of the base of every culture.

But there were exceptions. Some Lords had allowed their human societies to degenerate into dirt-indifference.

Anana had explained that the Lord of Earth was unique. Red Orc ruled in strictest secrecy and anonymity, although he had not always done so. In the early days, in man's dawn, he had often acted as a god. But he had abandoned that role and gone into hiding – as it were. He had let things go as they would. This accounted for the past, present, and doubtless future mess in which Earthlings were mired.

Kickaha had had little time to learn much about Red Orc, because he had not even known of his existence until a few minutes before he and Anana stepped through the gates into this universe.

'They all looked so ugly,' Anana said.

'I told you man had gone to seed here,' he said. 'There has been no selective breeding, either by a Lord or by humans themselves.'

Then they heard the muted roar of the cycles again, and in a minute they saw eight coming back up the road. These held only men.

The cycles passed them, slowed, turned, and came up behind them. Kickaha and Anana continued walking. Three cycles zoomed by them, cutting in so close that he could have knocked them over as they went by. He was beginning to wonder if he should not have done so and therefore cut down the odds immediately. It seemed obvious that they were going to be harassed, if not worse.

Some of the men whistled at Anana and called out invitations, or wishes, in various obscene terms. Anana did not understand the words but she understood the tones and gestures and grins that went with them. She scowled and made a gesture peculiar to the Lords. Despite their unfamiliarity with it, the cyclists understood. One almost fell off his cycle laughing. Others, however, bared their teeth in half-grins, half-snarls.

Kickaha stopped and faced them. They pulled up around the pair in an enfolding crescent and turned off their motors.

'OK,' Kickaha said. 'What do you want?'

A big-paunched, thick-necked youth with thick coarse black hair spilling out of the V of his shirt and wearing a goatee and an Afrika Korps hat, spoke up. 'Well, now, Red, if we was Satan's Slaves, we'd want you. But we ain't fags, so we'll take your *la belle dame con, voila.*'

'Man, that chick is the most!' said a tall skinny boy with acne scars, big Adam's apple, and a gold ring in a pierced ear. His long lank black hair hung down past his shoulders and fell over his eyes.

'The grooviest!' a bushy-bearded gap-toothed scar-faced man said.

Kickaha knew when to keep silent and when to talk, but he sometimes had a hard time doing what he knew was best. He had no time or inclination for brawls now; his business was serious and important. In fact, it was vital. If the Beller got loose and adapted to Earth well enough to make other bells, he and his kind would literally take over Earth. The Beller was no science-fiction monster; he existed, and if he were not killed, good-bye Earth! Or good-bye mankind! The bodies would survive but the brains would be emptied and alien minds would fill them.

It was unfortunate that salvation could not discriminate. If others were saved, then these would be too.

At the moment, it looked as if there could be some doubt about Kickaha being able to save even himself, let alone the world. The eight had left their cycles and were approaching with various weapons. Three had long chains; two, iron pipes; one, a switchblade knife; one, brass knuckles; another, an ice pick.

'I suppose you think you're going to attack her in broad daylight and with the cops so close?' he said.

The youth with the Afrika Korps cap said, 'Man, we wouldn't bother you, ordinarily. But when I saw that chick! it was too much! What a doll! I ain't never seen a chick could wipe her. Too much! We gotta have her. You dig?"

Kickaha did not understand what this last meant but it did not matter. They were brutal men who meant to have what they wanted.

"You better be prepared to die,' Kickaha said.

They looked surprised. The Afrika Korps youth said, 'You got a lotta class, Red, I'll give you that. Listen, we could stomp the guts outta you and enjoy it, really dig it, but I admire your style, friend. Let us have the chick, and we return her in an hour or so.'

Then Afrika Korps grinned and said, "Course, she may not be in the same condition she is now, but what the hell. Nobody's perfect!'

Kickaha spoke to Anana in the language of the Lords.

'If we get a chance, we'll make off on one of these cycles. It'll get us to Los Angeles.'

'Hey, what kinda gook talk is that?' Afrika Korps said. He gestured at the men with the chains, who, grinning, stepped in front of the others. They drew their arms back to lash out with the chains and Kickaha and Anana sprayed the beams from their rings, which were set at 'stun' power. The three dropped their chains, grabbed their middles, and bent over. The rays caught them on the tops of the heads then, and they fell forward. Their faces were red with suddenly broken blood vessels. When they recovered, they would be dizzy and sick for days and their stomachs would be sore and red with ruptured veins and arteries.

The others became motionless and went white with shock.

Kickaha snatched the knife out of his sheath and threw

it at the shoulder of Afrika Korps. Afrika Korps screamed and dropped the ice pick. Anana knocked him out with her ray; Kickaha sprayed the remaining men.

Fortunately, no cars came by in the next few minutes. The two dragged the groaning half-conscious men to the edge of the road and pushed them over. They rolled about twenty feet and came to rest on a shelf of rock.

The cycles, except for one, were then pushed over the edge at a place where there was nothing to stop them. They leaped and rolled down the steep incline, turned over and over, came apart, and some burst into flames.

Kickaha regretted this, since he did not want the smoke to attract anybody.

Anana had been told what the group had planned for her. She climbed down the slope to the piled-up bodies. She set the ring at the lowest burn power and burned off the pants, and much outer skin, of every male. They would not forget Anana for a long time. And if they cursed her in aftertimes, they should have blessed Kickaha. He kept her from killing them.

Kickaha took the wallet of Afrika Korps. The driver's licence gave his name as Alfred Roger Goodrich. His photograph did not look at all like Kickaha, which could not be helped. Among other things it contained forty dollars.

He instructed Anana in how to ride behind him and what to expect when they were on the road. Within a minute, they were out on the highway, heading toward Los Angeles. The roar of the engine did not resurrect the happy memories of his cycling days in Indiana. The road disturbed him and the reek of gasoline and oil displeased him. He had been in a quiet and sweet-aired world too long.

Anana, clinging to his waist, was silent for a long while. He glanced back once to see her black hair flying. Her lids were half-shut behind the sunglasses she had taken from one of the Louts. The shadows made them impenetrable. Later, she shouted something at him but the wind and the engine noise flicked her words away.

Kickaha tested the cycle out and determined that a number of items had been cut out by the owner, mostly to reduce weight. For one thing, the front brakes had been taken off.

Once he knew what the strengths and weaknesses of the vehicle were, he drove along with his eyes inspecting the road ahead but his thoughts inclined to be elsewhere.

He had come on a long and fantastic road from that campus of the University of Indiana to this road in the mountains of southern California. When he was with the Eighth Army in Germany, he had found that crescent of hard silvery metal in the ruins of a local museum. He took it back with him to Bloomington, and there, one night, a man by the name of Vannax had appeared and offered him a fantastic sum for the crescent. He had refused the money. Later that night he had awakened to find Vannax had broken into his apartment. Vannax was in the act of placing another crescent of metal by his to form a circle. Kickaha had attacked Vannax and accidentally stepped within the circle. The next he knew, he was transported to a very strange place.

The two crescents had formed the gate, a device of the Lords which permitted a sort of teleportation from one universe to another. Kickaha had been transmitted into an artificial universe, a pocket universe, created by a Lord named Jadawin. But Jadawin was no longer in his universe; he had been forced out of it by another Lord, dispossessed and cast into Earth. Jadawin had lost his memory. He became Robert Wolff.

The stories of Wolff (Jadawin) and Kickaha (Finnegan) were long and involved. Wolff was helped back into his universe by Kickaha, and, after a series of adventures, Wolff regained his memory. He also regained his Lordship of the peculiar universe he had constructed, and he settled down with his lover, Chryseis, to rule in the palace on top of the Tower-of-Babel-like planet which hung in the middle of a universe whose 'walls' contained a volume less than that within the solar system of Earth.

Recently, Wolff and Chryseis had mysteriously disappeared, probably because of the machinations of some

Lord of another universe. Kickaha had run into Anana, who, with two other Lords, was fleeing from the Black Bellers. The Bellers had originally been devices created in the biolabs of the Lords and intended for housing of the minds of the Lords during mind transference from one body to another. But the bell-shaped and indestructible machines had developed into entities with their own intelligence. These had succeeded in transferring their minds into the bodies of Lords and then began to wage a secret war on the Lords. They were found out, and a long and savage struggle began, with all the Bellers supposedly captured and imprisoned in a specially made universe. However, fifty-one had been overlooked, and these, after ten thousand years of dormancy, had gotten into human bodies again and were once more loose.

Kickaha had directly or indirectly killed all but one. This one, its mind in the body of a man called Thabuuz, had gated through to Earth. Wolff and Chryseis had returned to their palace just in time to be attacked by the Bellers and had escaped through the gate which Thabuuz later took.

Now Kickaha and Anana were searching for Wolff and Chryseis. And they were also determined to hunt down and kill the last of the Black Bellers. If Thabuuz succeeded in eluding them, he would, in time, build more of the bells and with these begin a secret war against the humans of Earth, and, later, invade the private universes of the Lords and discharge their minds and occupy their bodies also. The Lords had never forgotten the Black Bellers, and every one still wore a ring which could detect the metal bells of their ancient enemies and transmit a warning to a tiny circuit-board and alarm in the brain of every Lord.

The peoples of Earth knew nothing of the Bellers. They knew nothing of the Lords. Kickaha was the only Earthling who had ever become aware of the existence of the Lords and their pocket universes.

The peoples of Earth would be wide open to being taken over, one by one, their minds discharged by the antennas of the bells and the minds of the Bellers possessing the brains. The warfare would be so insidious that only through accident would the humans even know that they were being attacked.

The Black Beller Thabuuz had to be found and killed.

In the meantime, the Lord of Earth, the Lord called Red Orc, had learned that five people had gated through into his domain. He would not know that one of them was the Black Beller. He would be trying to capture all five. And Red Orc could not be notified that a Black Beller was loose on Earth because Red Orc could not be found. Neither Anana nor Kickaha knew where he lived. Indeed, until a few hours ago, Kickaha had not known that Earth had a Lord.

In fifteen minutes, they had come down off the slope onto a plateau. The little village at the crossroads was a pleasant place, though highly commercialized. It was clean and bright with many white houses and buildings. However, as they passed through the main street, they passed a big hamburger stand. And there was the rest of Lucifer's Louts lounging by the picnic tables, eating hamburgers and drinking cokes or beer. They looked up on hearing the familiar Harley-Davidson and then, seeing the two, did a double take. One jumped onto his cycle and kicked over the motor. He was a tall frowzy-haired long-moustachioed youth wearing a Confederate officer's cavalry hat, white silk shirt with frills at the neck and wrists, tight black shiny pants with red seams, and fur-topped boots.

The others quickly followed him. Kickaha did not think they would be going to the police; there was something about them which indicated that their relations with the police were not friendly. They would take vengeance in their own dirty hands. However, it was not likely that they would do anything while still in town.

Kickaha accelerated to top speed.

When they had gone around a curve which took them out of sight of the village, Anana half-turned. She waited until the leader was only ten feet behind her. He was bent over the bars and grinning savagely. Evidently he expected to pass them and either force them to stop or to knock them over. Behind him, side by side so that two rode in the other lane, were five cycles with individual riders. The engines burdened down with couples were some twenty yards behind.

Kickaha glanced back and yelled at Anana. She released the ray just long enough to cut the front wheel of the lead cycle in half. Its front dropped, and the rider shot over the bars, his mouth open in a yell no one could hear. He hit the macadam and slid for a long way on his face and body. The five cycles behind him tried to avoid the first, which lay in their path. They split like a school of fish, but Anana cut the wheels of the two in the lead and all three piled up while two skidded on their sides off the road. The other cycles slowed down in time to avoid hitting the fallen engines and drivers.

Kickaha grinned and shouted, 'Good show, Anana!'

And then his grin fell off and he cursed. Around the corner of the road, now a half-mile away, a black and white car with red lights on top had appeared. Any hopes that he had that it would stop to investigate the accident quickly faded. The car swung to the shoulder to avoid the fallen vehicles and riders and then twisted back onto the road and took off after Kickaha, its siren whooping, its red lights flashing.

The car was about fifty yards away when Anana swept the ray down the road and across the front tyres. She snapped the ray off so quickly that the wheels were probably only disintegrated a little on the rims, but the tyres were cut in two. The car dropped a little but kept going on, though it decreased speed so suddenly that the two policemen were thrown violently forward. The siren died; the lights quit flashing; the car shook to a halt. And Kickaha and Anana sped around a curve and saw the policemen no more.

'If this keeps up, we're going to be out of charges!' Kickaha said. 'Hell, I wanted to save them for extreme emergencies! I didn't think we'd be having so much trouble so soon! And we're just started!'

They continued for five miles and then he saw another

police car coming towards them. It went down a dip and was lost for a minute. He shouted, 'Hang on' and swung off the road, bouncing across a slight depression towards a wide field that grew more rocks than grass. His goal was a clump of trees about a hundred yards away, and he almost made it before the police came into view. Anana, hanging on, yelled that the police car was coming across the field after them. Kickaha slowed the cycle. Anana ran the ray down the field in front of the advancing car. Burning dirt flew up in dust along a furrow and then the tyres exploded and the front of the radiator of the car gushed water and steam.

Kickaha took the cycle back towards the road at an angle away from the car. Two policemen jumped out and, steadying their pistols, fired. The chances of hitting the riders of the machine at that distance were poor, but a bullet did penetrate the rear tyre. There was a bang; the cycle began fishtailing. Kickaha cut the motor, and they coasted to a stop. The policemen began running towards them.

'Hell, I don't want to kill them!' Kickaha said. 'But...'

The policemen were big and blubbery-looking and looked as if they might be between forty and fifty years old. Kickaha and Anana were wearing packs of about thirty pounds, but both were physically about twenty-five years old.

'We'll outrun them,' he said, and they fled together towards the road. The two men fired their guns and shouted but they were slowing down swiftly and soon they were trotting. A half-mile later, they were standing together watching the two dwindle.

Kickaha, grinning, circled back towards the car. He looked back once and saw that the two policemen realized that he had led them astray. They were running again but not too swiftly. Their legs and arms were pumping at first but soon the motions became less energetic, and then both were walking towards him.

Kickaha opened the door to the car, tore off the microphone of the transceiver, reached under the dashboard and tore loose all the wires connected to the radio. By that time, Anana had caught up with him.

The keys were still in the ignition lock, and the wheels themselves had not been cut into deeply. He told Anana to jump in, and he got behind the driver's wheel and started the motor. The cops speeded up then and began firing again, but the car pulled away from them and bumped and shook across the field, accelerating all the time. One bullet pierced and starred a rear window, and then the car was bump-bumping down the road.

After two miles of the grinding noise and piston-like movement, Kickaha decided to call it quits. He drove the car to the side of the road, got out, threw the ignition keys into the weeds, and started to hike again. They had walked perhaps fifty yards when they turned at the noise of a vehicle. A bus shot by them. It was painted all over with swirls, dots, squares, circles, and explosions of many bright colours. In bright yellow and orange-trimmed letters was a title along the front and the sides of the bus: THE GNOME KING AND HIS BAD EGG. Above the title were painted glowing red and yellow quarter notes, bars, small guitars and drums.

For a moment, looking at the faces against the windows, he thought that the bus had picked up Lucifer's Louts. There were long hairs, fuzzy hairs, moustaches, beards, and the heavy make-up and long straight lank hair of the girls.

The bus slowed down with a squealing of brakes. It stopped, a door swung open, and a youth with a beard and enormous spectacles leaned out and waved at them. They ran to the bus and boarded with the accompaniment of much laughter and the strumming of guitars.

The bus, driven by a youth who looked like Buffalo Bill, started up. Kickaha looked around into the grinning faces of six boys and three girls. Three older men sat at the rear of the bus and played cards on a small collapsible table. They looked up and nodded and then went back to their game. Part of the bus was enclosed; there were, he later found out, a toilet and washroom and two small dressing rooms. Guitars, drums, xylophone, saxophone, flute, and harp, were stored on seats or on the racks above the seats.

Two girls wore skirts that just barely covered their buttocks and dark grey stockings, bright frilly blouses, many varicoloured beads, and heavy make-up: green or silver eyelids, artificial eyelashes, panda-like rings around the eyes, and green (!) and pale mauve (!) lips. The third girl had no make-up at all. Long straight black hair fell to her waist and she wore a tight sleeveless green and red striped sweater with a deep cleavage, tight levis, and sandals. Several of the boys wore bellbottom trousers, very frilly shirts, and all had long hair.

The Gnome King was a very tall, tubercular looking youth with very curly hair, handlebar moustache, and enormous spectacles perched on the end of his big nose. He also wore an earring. He introduced himself as Lou Baum (born Goldbaum).

Kickaha gave his name as Paul Finnegan and Anana's as Ann Finnegan. She was his wife, he told Baum, and had only recently come from Finnish Lapland. He gave this pedigree because he did not think that it was likely they would run into anyone who could speak Laplander.

'From the Land of the Reindeer?' Baum said. 'She's a dear, all right.' He whistled and kissed his fingertips and flicked them at Anana. 'Groovy, me boy! Too much! Say, either of you play an instrument?' He looked at the case Kickaha was carrying.

Kickaha said that they did not. He did not care to explain that he had once played the flute but not since 1945 or that he had played an instrument like a pan-pipe when he lived with the Bear Folk on the Amerindian level of the World of Tiers. Nor did he think it wise to explain that Anana played a host of instruments, some of which were similar to Earth instruments and some of which were definitely not.

'I'm using this instrument case as a suitcase,' Kickaha said. 'We've been on the road for some time since leaving Europe. We just spent a month in the mountains, and now we've decided to visit L.A. We've never been there.'

'Then you got no place to stay,' Baum said. He talked

to Kickaha but stared at Anana. His eyes glistened, and his hands kept moving with gestures that seemed to be reshaping Anana out of the air.

'Can she sing?' he said suddenly.

'Not in English,' Kickaha replied.

The girl in levis stood up and said, 'Come on, Lou. You aren't going to get anywhere with that chick. Her boy friend'll kill you if you lay a hand on her. Or else she will. That chick can do it, you know.'

Lou seemed to be shaken. He came very close and peered into Kickaha's eyes as if he were looking through a microscope. Kickaha smelled a strange acrid odour on his breath. A moment later, he thought he knew what it was. The citizens of the city of Talanac on the Amerind level, carved out of a mountain of jade, smoked a narcotic tobacco which left the same odour on their breath. Kickaha did not know, of course, since he had had no experience on Earth, but he had always suspected that the tobacco was marijuana, and that the Talanacs, descendants of the ancient Olmecs of Mexico, had brought it with them when they had crossed through the gates provided by Wolff.

'You wouldn't put me on?' Lou said to the girl, Moo-Moo Nanssen, after he had backed away from Kickaha's leaf-green eyes.

'There's something very strange about them,' Moo-Moo said. 'Very attractive, very virile, and very frightening. Alien. Real alien.'

Kickaha felt the back of his scalp chill. Anana, moving closer to him, whispered in the language of the Lords, 'I don't know what she's saying, but I don't like it. That girl has a gift of seeing things; she is *zundra*.'

Zundra had no exact or near-exact translation into English. It meant a combination of psychologist, clairvoyant, and witch, with a strain of madness.

Lou Baum shook his head, wiped the sweat off his forehead, and then removed and polished his glasses. His weak, pale-blue eyes blinked.

'The chick is psychic,' he said. 'Weird. But in the groove. She knows what she's talking about.'

'I get vibrations,' Moo-Moo said. 'They never fail me. I can read character like that!' She snapped her fingers loudly. 'But there's something about you two, especially her, I don't get. Maybe like you two ain't from this world, you know. Like you're Martians . . . or something.'

A short stocky youth with blond hair and an acne-scarred face, introduced only as Wipe-Out, looked up from his seat, where he was tuning a guitar.

'Finnegan's no Martian,' he said, grinning. 'He's got a flat Midwestern accent like he came from Indiana, Illinois, or Iowa. A hoosier, I'd guess. Right?'

'I'm a hoosier,' Kickaha said.

'Close your eyes, you good people,' Wipe-Out said loudly. 'Listen to him! Speak again, Finnegan! If his voice isn't a dead ringer for Gary Cooper's, I'll eat the inedible!'

Kickaha said something for their benefit, and the others laughed and said, 'Gary Cooper! Did you ever?'

That seemed to shatter the crystal tension that Moo-Moo's words had built. Moo-Moo smiled and sat down again, but her dark eyes flicked glances again and again at the two strangers, and Kickaha knew that she was not satisfied. Lou Baum sat down by Moo-Moo. His Adam's apple worked as if it were the plunger on a pump. His face was set in a heavy, almost stupefied expression, but Kickaha could tell that he was still very curious. He was also afraid.

Apparently, Baum believed in his girl friend's reputation as a psychic. He was also probably a little afraid of her.

Kickaha did not care. Her analysis of the strangers may have been nothing but a manoeuvre to scare Baum from Anana.

The important thing was to get to Los Angeles as swiftly as possible, with as little chance of being detected by Orc's men as possible. This bus was a lucky thing for him, and as soon as they reached a suitable jumping-off place in the metropolitan area, they would jump. And hail and farewell to the Gnome King and His Bad Eggs.

He inspected the rest of the bus. The three older men playing cards looked up at him but said nothing. He felt a little repulsed by their bald heads and grey hair, their thickening and sagging features, red-veined eyes, wrinkles, dewlaps, and big bellies. He had not seen more than four old people in the twenty-four years he had lived in the universe of Jadawin. Humans lived to be a thousand there, if they could avoid accident or homicide, and did not age until the last hundred years. Very few survived that long, however. Thus, Kickaha had forgotten about old men and women. He felt repelled, though not as much as Anana. She had grown up in a world which contained no physically aged people, and though she was now ten thousand years old, she had lived in no universes which contained unhandsome humans. The Lords were an aesthetic people and so they had weeded out the unbeautiful among their chattel and given the survivors the chance for a long long youth.

Baum walked down the aisle and said, 'Looking for something?'

'I'm just curious,' Kickaha said. 'Is there any way out other than the door in front.'

'There's an emergency inside the women's dressing room? Why?'

'I just like to know these things,' Kickaha said. He did not see why he should explain that he always made sure he knew exactly the number of exits and their accessibility.

He opened the doors to the two dressing rooms and the toilet and then studied the emergency door so that he would be able to open it immediately.

Baum, behind him, said, 'You sure got guts, friend. Didn't you know curiosity killed the cat.'

'It's kept this cat alive,' Kickaha said.

Baum lowered his voice and came close to Kickaha. He said, 'You really hung up on that chick?'

The phrase was new to Kickaha but he had no trouble understanding it.

He said, 'Yes. Why?'

'Too bad. I've really flipped for her. No offence, you understand,' he said when Kickaha narrowed his eyes. Moo-Moo's a real doll, but a little weird, you know what I mean. She says you two are weirdos, and there is something a little strange about you, but I like that. But I was going to say, if you need some money, say one or two thousand, and you'd just, say, give me a deed to your chick, in a manner of speaking, let me take over, and walk out, much richer, you know what I mean.'

Kickaha grinned and said, 'Two thousand? You must want her pretty bad!'

'Two thousand doesn't grow on the money tree, my friend, but for that doll . . .!'

'Your business must be very good, if you can throw that much away,' Kickaha said.

'Man, you kidding!' Baum said, seemingly genuinely surprised. 'Ain't you really heard of me and my group before? We're famous! We've been everywhere, we've made the top ten thirty-eight times, we got a Golden Record, we've given concerts at the Bowl! And we're on our way to the Bowl again. You don't seem to be with it!'

'I've been away for a long time,' Kickaha said. 'So what if I take your money and Ann doesn't fall for you? I can't force her to become your woman, you know.'

Baum seemed offended. He said, 'The chicks offer themselves to me by the dozens every night. I'm not jesting. I got the pick! You saying this Ann, Daughter-of-Reindeer, or whatever her name, is going to turn *me* down? Baum, the Gnome King?'

Baum's features were not only unharmonious, he had several pimples, and his teeth were crooked.

'Do you have the money on you?'

Baum's voice had been questioning, even wheedling before. Now it became triumphant and, at the same time, slightly scornful.

'I can give you a thousand; maybe Solly, my agent, can give you five hundred. And I'll give you a cheque for the rest.'

'White slavery!' Kickaha said. And then, 'You can't be over twenty-five, right? And you can throw money around like that?'

He remembered his own youth during the Depression

and how hard he had worked to just survive and how tough so many others had had it.

'You are a weirdo,' Baum said. 'Don't you know anything? Or are you putting me on?'

His voice was loaded with contempt. Kickaha felt like laughing in his face and also felt like hitting him in his mouth. He did neither. He said, I'll take the fifteen hundred. But right now. And if Ann spits on you, you don't get the money back.'

Baum glanced nervously at Moo-Moo, who had moved over to sit with Anana.

He said, 'Wait till we get to L.A. We'll stop off to eat, and then you can take off. I'll give you your money then.'

'And you can get up your nerve to tell Moo-Moo that Ann is joining you but I'm taking off?' Kickaha said. 'Very well. Except for the money. I want it now! Otherwise, I tell Moo-Moo what you just said.'

Baum turned a little pale and his undershot jaw sagged. He said, 'You slimy . . .! You got a nerve!'

'You think I'd double-cross you, turn you in to the fuzz?'

'And I want a signed statement explaining why I'm getting the money. Any legitimate excuse will do.'

'That possibility did cross my mind,' Kickaha said, wondering if the 'fuzz' was the police.

'You may have been out of it for a long time, but you haven't forgotten any of the tricks, have you?' Baum said, not so scornfully now.

'There are people like you every place,' Kickaha said.

He knew that he and Anana would need money, and they had no time to go to work to earn it, and he did not want to rob to get it if he could avoid doing so. If this nauseating specimen of arrogance thought he could buy Anana, let him pay for the privilege of finding out whether or not he could.

Baum dug into his jacket and came up with eight one-hundred dollar bills. He handed these to Kickaha and then interrupted his manager, a fat bald-headed man with a huge cigar. The manager gestured violently and shot some hard looks at Kickaha but he gave in. Baum came back with five one-hundred dollar bills. He wrote a note on a piece of paper, saying that the money was in payment for a debt he owed Paul J. Finnegan. After giving it to Kickaha, he insisted that Kickaha write him a receipt for the money. Kickaha also took the cheque for the rest of the money, although he did not think that he would be able to cash it. Baum would stop payment on it, he was sure of that.

Kickaha left Baum and sat down on a seat on which was a number of magazines, paperback books, and a *Los Angeles Times.* He spent some time reading, and when he had finished he sat for a long time looking out the window.

Earth had certainly changed since 1946.

Pulling himself out of his reverie, he picked up a road map of Los Angeles, which he'd noticed among the magazines. As he studied it, he realized Wolff and Chryseis could be anywhere in the great sprawl of Los Angeles. He was certain they were headed in that direction, though, rather than Nevada or Arizona, since the nearest gate was in the L.A. area. They might even be in a bus only a few miles ahead.

Since Wolff and Chryseis had taken the gate to Earth from the palace in Wolff's universe as an emergency exit to avoid being killed by the invaders, they were dressed in the clothes of the Lords. Chryseis may have been wearing no clothes at all. So the two would have been forced to obtain clothes from others. And they would have had to find some big dark glasses immediately, because anyone seeing Chryseis' enormous violet eyes would have known that she was not Earth-born. Or would have thought her a freak, despite her great beauty.

Both of them were resourceful enough to get along, especially since Wolff had spent more time on Earth as an adult than Kickaha had.

As for the Beller, he would be in an absolutely strange and frightening world. He could speak no word of the language, and he would want to cling to his bell, which would be embarrassing and inconvenient for him. But he could have gone in any direction.

The only thing Kickaha could do was to head toward

the nearest known gate in the hope that Wolff and Chryseis would also be doing that. If they met there, they could team up, consider what to do next, and plan on the best way of locating the Beller. If Wolff and Chryseis did not show, then everything would be up to Kickaha.

Moo-Moo sat down by him. She put her hand on his arm and said, 'My, you're muscular!'

'I have a few,' he said, grinning. 'Now that you've softened me up with your comments on my hardness, what's on your mind?'

She leaned against him, rubbing the side of her large breast against his arm, and said, 'That Lou! He sees a new chick that's reasonably good-looking, and he flips every time. He's been talking to you, trying to get you to give your girl friend to him, hasn't he? I'll bet he offered you money for her?'

'Some,' Kickaha said. 'What about it?'

She felt the muscles of his thigh and said, 'Two can play at that game.'

'You offering me money, too' he said.

She drew away from him, her eyes widening and then she said, 'You're putting me on! *I* should pay *you*?'

At another time, Kickaha might have played the game out to the end. But, corny as it sounded, the fate of the human race on Earth really depended on him. If the Beller adjusted to this world, and succeeded in making other bells, and then the minds in these possessed the bodies of human beings, the time would come when . . . Moo-Moo herself would become a mindless thing and then a body and brain inhabited by another entity.

It might not matter, however. If he were to believe half of what he read in the magazines and newspaper, the human race might well have doomed itself. And all life on the planet. Earth might be better off with humans occupied by the minds of Bellers. Bellers were logical beings, and, given a chance they would clear up the mess that humans seemed to have made of the entire planet.

Kickaha shuddered a little. Such thinking was dangerous.

There could be no rest until the last of the Bellers died.

"What's the matter with you?' Moo-Moo said, her voice losing its softness. 'You don't dig me.'

He patted her thigh and said, 'You're a beautiful woman, Moo-Moo, but I love Ann. However, tell you what! If the Gnome King succeeds in turning Ann into one of his Bad Eggs, you and I will make music together. And it won't be the cacophony that radio is vomiting.'

She jerked with surprise and then said, 'What do you mean? That's the Rolling Stones!'

'No moss gathered here,' he said.

'You're not with it,' she said. 'Man, you're square, square, square! You sure you're not over thirty?'

He shrugged. He had not cared for the popular music of his youth, either. But it was sometimes pleasant, when compared to this screeching rhythm which turned his teeth in on himself.

The bus had moved out of the desert country into greener land. It sped along the freeway despite the increasing traffic. The sun was shining down so fiercely now, and the air was hot. The air was also noisy with the roar of cars and stinking with fumes. His eyes stung, and the insides of his nostrils felt needled. A greyish haze was lying ahead; then they were in it, and the air seemed to clear somewhat, and the haze was ahead again.

Moo-Moo said something about the smog really being fierce this time of the year and especially along here. Kickaha had read about smog in one of the magazines, although he did not know the origin of the word as yet. If this was what the people of southern California lived in, he wanted no more to do with it. Anana's eyes were red and teary, and she was sniffling and complaining of a headache and clogging sinuses.

Moo-Moo left him, and Anana sat down by him.

'You never said anything about this when you were describing your world to me,' she said.

'I didn't know anything about it,' he said. 'It developed after I left Earth.'

The bus had been travelling swiftly and too wildly. It

had switched lanes back and forth as it squeezed between cars, tailgating and cutting in ahead madly. The driver crouched over his wheel, his eyes seeming to blaze, his mouth hanging open and his tongue flicking out. He paid no attention to the sound of screeching brakes and blaring horns, but leaned on his own horn when he wanted to scare somebody just ahead of him. The horn was very loud and deep and must have sounded like a locomotive horn to many a startled driver. These usually pulled over to another lane, sometimes doing it so swiftly, they almost sideswiped other cars.

After a while, the press of cars was so heavy that the bus was forced to crawl along or even stop now and then. For miles ahead, traffic was creeping along. The heat and the grey haze thickened.

Moo-Moo said to Baum, 'Why can't we get air conditioning on this bus? We certainly make enough money!'

'How often do we get on the freeway?' the manager said.

Kickaha told Anana about Baum's proposal.

Anana said, 'I don't know whether to laugh or to throw up.'

'A little of both might help you,' he said. 'Well, I promised I wouldn't try to argue you out of it if you decided to take him in preference to me. Which, by the way, he seemed one hundred percent sure would happen.'

'You sell me; you worry a while until I make up my mind,' she said.

'Sure. I'll do that,' he replied. He rose and sauntered down the aisle and looked out the back of the bus. After a while he came back and sat down again with Anana.

In a low voice, he said, 'There's a big black Lincoln Continental, I believe, behind us. I recognized one of the men in it. I saw him through the binoculars when I looked down from the cave.'

'How could they have found us?' she said. Her voice was steady but her body was rigid.

'Maybe they didn't,' he said. 'It might be just a coincidence. They may have no idea they're so close to us. And then, again . . .'

It did not seem at all likely. But how had they caught up with them? Had they been posted along the road and seen them go by in the bus? Or did Orc have such a widespread organization that someone on the bus had reported to him?

He dismissed this last thought as sheer paranoia. Only time would show whether or not it was coincidence.

So far, the men in the car had not seemed interested in the bus. They were having a vigorous dispute. Three of them were dark and between forty and fifty-five years old. The fourth was a young man with blond hair cut in a Julius Caesar style. Kickaha studied them until he had branded their features on his mind. Then he returned to the seat near the front.

After a while, the traffic speeded up. The bus sped by grim industrial sections and the back ends of run-down buildings. The greyish green-tinged smog did not thicken, but its corrosive action became worse. Anana said, 'Do your people live in this all the time? They must be very tough!'

'You know as much as I do about it,' he said.

Baum suddenly rose from his seat beside Moo-Moo and said to the driver, 'Jim, when you get near Civic Centre, pull off and look for a hamburger stand. I'm hungry.'

The others protested. They could eat at the hotel when they got there. It would only take about a half hour more. What was his hurry?

'I'm hungry!' he shouted. He looked wild-eyed at them and stomped his foot hard. 'I'm hungry! I don't want to wait any longer! Besides, if we got to fight our way through the usual mob of teenyboppers, we may be held up for some time! Let's eat now!'

The others shrugged. Evidently they had seen him act this way before. He looked as if he were going to scream and stamp through the floor, like in a tantrum, if he did not get his way.

It was not a whim this time, however. Moo-Moo rolled her eyes and then came up to Kickaha and said, 'He's letting you know it's time to bow out, Red. You better take your worldly goods and kiss your girl friend good-bye.'

'You've been through this before?' Kickaha said, grinning. 'What makes you so sure Ann'll be staying?'

'I'm not so sure about her,' Moo-Moo said. 'I sensed something weird about you two, and the feeling hasn't gone away. In fact, it's even stronger.'

She surprised Kickaha then by saying, 'You two are running away, aren't you? From the fuzz. And from others. More than the fuzz. Somebody close behind you now. I smell danger.'

She squeezed his arm, bent lower, and whispered, 'If I can help you, I'll be at the Beverly Hilton for a week, then we go to San Francisco. You call me. I'll tell the hotel to let you through. Any time.'

Kickaha felt warmed by her interest and offer of help. At the same time, he could not keep from considering that she might know more than any would-be friend of his should. Was it possible that she was tied in with Red Orc?

He rejected that. His life had been so full of danger, one perilous situation after another, and he had gotten into the prosurvival habit of always considering the worst and planning possible actions to avoid it. In this case, Moo-Moo could be nothing more than a psychic, or, at least, a very sensitive person.

The bus pulled off the freeway and drove to the Music Centre. Kickaha would have liked to study the tall buildings here, which reminded him of those of Manhattan, but he was watching the big black Lincoln and its four occupants. It had turned when the bus turned and was now two cars behind. Kickaha was willing to concede that its getting off the freeway here might be another coincidence. But he doubted it very much.

The bus pulled into a corner of a parking lot in the centre of which was a large hamburger stand. The bus doors opened, and the driver got out first. Baum took Anana's hand and led her out. Kickaha noted this out of the corner of his eye; he was watching the Lincoln. It had pulled into a parking place five cars down from the stand.

Baum was immediately surrounded by five or six young girls who shrieked his name and a number of unintelligible exclamations. They also tried to touch him. Baum smiled at them and waved his hands for them to back away. After a minute's struggle, he and the older men succeeded in backing them off.

Kickaha, carrying the instrument case, followed Moo-Moo off the bus and across the lot to the picnic table under a shady awning, where Baum and Anana were seated. The waitress brought hamburgers, hot dogs, milk shakes, and cokes. He salivated when he saw his hamburger. It had been, God, over twenty-four years since he had tasted a hamburger! He bit down and then chewed slowly. There was something in the meat, some unidentified element, that he did not like. This distasteful substance also seemed to be in the lettuce and the tomato.

Anana grimaced and said, in the language of the Lords, 'What do you put in this food?'

Kickaha shrugged and said, 'Insecticide, maybe, although it doesn't seem possible that we could detect one part in a million or whatever it was. Still, there's something.'

They fared better with the chocolate milk shake. This was as thick and creamy and delicious as he remembered it. Anana nodded her approval, too.

The men were still in the Lincoln and were looking at him and Anana. At the group, anyway.

Baum looked across to Kickaha and said, 'OK, Finnegan. This is it. Take off!'

Kickaha glanced up at him and said, 'The bargain was, I take off if she agrees to go with you.'

Baum laughed and said, 'Just trying to spare your feelings, my Midwestern rustic. But have it your way. Watch me, maybe you'll learn something.'

He leaned over Anana, who was talking with Moo-Moo. Moo-Moo glanced once at Baum's face, then got up, and walked off. Kickaha watched Baum and Anana. The conversation was short; the action, abrupt and explosive.

Anana slapped Baum so hard across the face that its noise could be heard above the gabble of his fans and the roar of the traffic. There was a short silence from everybody around Baum and then a number of shrieks of anger from the girl fans. Baum shouted angrily and swung with his right fist at Anana. She dodged and slid off the bench, but then the people around her blocked Kickaha's view.

He scooped off some change on the table, left by customers. Putting this in his pocket, he jumped into the fray. He was, however, almost knocked down by the press of bodies trying to get away. The girls rammed into him, clawed at him, shrieked, gouged, and kicked.

Suddenly, there was an opening. He saw Baum lying on the cement, his legs drawn up and his hands clenching his groin. A girl, bent over, was sitting by him and holding her stomach. Another girl was leaning over a wooden table, her back to him and retching.

Kickaha grabbed Anana's hand and shouted, 'Come on! This is the chance we've been looking for!'

The instrument case in his other hand, he led her running towards the back of the parking lot. Just before they went down a narrow alley between two tall buildings, he looked back. The car containing his shadowers had pulled into the lot, and three of the men were getting out. They saw their quarry, and ran toward them. But they were not stupid enough to pull out weapons before they caught up with them. Kickaha did not intend that they should catch up with them.

And then, as he ran out of the alley and into the next street, he thought, *Why not? I could spend years trying to find Red Orc but if I can get hold of those who work for him . . . ?*

The next street was as busy as the one they had just left. The two stopped running but did walk swiftly. A police car, proceeding in the same direction, suddenly accelerated, its lights coming into red life. It took the corner with squealing tyres, pursued by the curses of an old man who looked like a wino.

He looked behind him. The three men were still following but making no effort to overtake them. One man was talking into something concealed in his hand. He was either speaking to the man in the car or to his boss. Kickaha understood by now that radio sets were much smaller than in 1946 and that the man might be using a quite common miniature transceiver. On the other hand, he might be using a device unknown on Earth except to those who worked for Red Orc.

They continued walking. He looked back once more when they had covered two blocks. The big black Lincoln had stopped, and the three men were getting into it. Kickaha halted before a pawn shop and looked through the dirty plate glass window at the backwash of people's hopes. He said, 'We'll give them a chance to try to pick us up. I don't know that they'll have guts enough to do it in broad daylight but if they do, here's what we do. . . .'

The Lincoln drew up even with them and stopped.

Kickaha turned around and grinned at the men in the Lincoln. The front and back doors on the right side opened, and three men got out. They walked toward the couple, their hands in their coat pockets. At that moment, a siren wailed down the street. The three jerked their heads to look at the police car which had suddenly appeared. It shot between cars, swerved sharply to cut around the Lincoln, and went on through the traffic light just as it was turning red. It kept on going; evidently it was not headed for the trouble around the corner.

The three men had turned casually and walked back toward the Lincoln. Kickaha took advantage of their concern over the police car. Before they could turn around again, he was behind them. He shoved his knuckles into the back of the oldest man and said, 'I'll burn a hole through you if you make any trouble.'

Anana had her ring finger against the back of the young man with the tangled blond hair. He stiffened, and his jaw dropped, as if he could not believe that not only had their hunted turned against them, they were doing so before at least fifty witnesses.

Horns started blaring at the Lincoln. The driver gestured at the three to hurry back, then he saw that Kickaha and Anana were pressed up closely against the backs of two of the men. The third man, who had overheard Kickaha, waved at the driver to go on. The Lincoln took off with a screeching and burning of tyres and swung around the corner without coming to a stop first.

'That was a smart move!' Kickaha said to the man just in front of him. 'One up for you!'

The third man began to walk away. Kickaha said, 'I'll kill this guy if you don't come back!'

'Kill him!' the man said and continued walking.

Kickaha spoke in Lord language to Anana. 'Let your man go! We'll keep this one and herd him to a private place where we can talk.'

'What's to keep the others from following us?'

'Nothing. I don't care at this moment if they do.'

He did, but he did not want the others to think so.

The blond sneered at them and swaggered off. There was something in his walk, however, which betrayed him. He was very relieved to have gotten away unhurt.

Kickaha then told the remaining man just what would happen if he tried to run away. The man said nothing. He seemed very calm. A genuine professional, Kickaha thought. It would have been better to have kept the blond youth, who might not be so tough to crack. It was too late to do anything about that, however.

The problem was: where to take the man for questioning? They were in the centre of a vast metropolis unfamiliar to either Kickaha or Anana. There should be some third-rate hotels around here, judging by the appearance of the buildings and many of the pedestrians. It might be possible to rent a room and interrogate their captive there. But he could ruin everything if he opened his mouth and screamed. And even if he could be gotten into a hotel room, his buddies would have trailed them there and would call in reinforcements. The hotel room would be a trap.

Kickaha gave the order and the three started walking. He was on one side of the man and Anana was on the other. He studied his captive's profile, which looked brutish but strong. The man was about fifty, had a dark sallow skin, brown eyes, a big curved nose, a thick mouth, and a massive chin. Kickaha asked his name, and the man growled, 'Mazarin.'

'Who do you work for?' Kickaha said.

'Somebody you'd better not mess around with,' Mazarin said.

'You tell me who your boss is and how I can get to him, and I'll let you go scot-free,' Kickaha said. 'Otherwise, I burn you until you tell. You know everybody has their limits, and you might be able to take a lot of burning, but you'll give in eventually.'

The man shrugged big shoulders and said, 'Sure. What about it?'

'Are you really that loyal?' Kickaha said.

The man looked at him contemptuously. 'No, but I don't figure you'll get the chance to do anything. And I don't intend to say anything more.'

He clamped his lips shut and turned his eyes away.

They had walked two blocks. Kickaha looked behind him. The Lincoln had come around and picked up the two men and now was proceeding slowly on the lane nearest the sidewalk.

Kickaha did not doubt that the three had gotten into contact with their boss and were waiting for reinforcements. It was an impasse.

Then he grinned again.

He spoke rapidly to Anana, and they directed Mazarin to the edge of the road. They waited until the Lincoln drew even and then stepped out. The three were staring from the car as if they could not believe what they were seeing. They also looked apprehensive. The car stopped when Kickaha waved at them. The two on the right side of the car had their guns out and pointed through the window, although their other hands concealed the barrels as best they could.

Kickaha pushed Mazarin ahead of him, and they walked around in front of the car and to the driver's side. Anana stopped on the right side of the car about five feet away.

Kickaha said, 'Get into the car!'

Mazarin looked at him with an unreadable expression. He opened the rear door and began to climb in. Kickaha shoved him on in and came in with him. At the same time,

Anana stepped up to the car. The driver had turned around and the other two had turned to watch Kickaha. She pressed the ring, which was set to stun power again, against the head of the man in the front right seat. He slumped over, and at the same time Kickaha stunned Mazarin.

The blond youth in the right rear seat pointed his gun at Kickaha and said, 'You must be outta your mind! Don't move or I'll plug you!'

The energy from the ring hit the back of his head and spread out over the bone of the skull, probably giving the skin a first-degree burn through all the layers of cells. His head jerked forward as if a fist had hit it; his finger jerked in reflex. The .38 automatic went off once, sounding loudly inside the car. Mazarin jerked, fell back, his arms flying out and his hand hitting Kickaha in the chest. Then he fell over, slowly, against Kickaha.

The driver yelled and gunned the car. Anana leaped back to keep from being run over. Kickaha shouted at the driver, but the man kept the accelerator pressed to the floor. He screamed back an obscenity. He intended to keep going, even through the red light ahead at the intersection, on the theory that Kickaha would be too frightened of the results if he knocked him out.

Kickaha stunned him anyway, and the car immediately slowed down. It did not stop, however, and so rolled into the rear end of a car waiting for the red light to change. Kickaha had squatted down on the floor behind the driver's seat to cushion the impact. He was thrown forward with the back of the seat and the driver's body taking up most of the energy.

Immediately thereafter, he opened the door and crawled out. The man in the car in front of him was still sitting in his seat, looking stunned. Kickaha reached back into the car and took out Mazarin's wallet from his jacket pocket. He then removed the driver's wallet. The registration card for the car was not on the steering wheel column nor was it in the glove compartment. He could not afford to spend any more time at the scene. Kickaha walked away and then began running when he heard a scream behind him.

He met Anana at the intersection, and they took a left turn around the corner. Only one man had pursued Kickaha, but he had halted when Kickaha had glared at him, and he did not continue his dogging.

He hailed a cab, and they climbed in. Remembering the map of Los Angeles he had studied on the bus, he ordered the driver to drop them off on Lorraine, south of Wilshire.

Anana did not ask him what he was doing because he had told her to keep quiet. He did not want the cab driver to remember a woman who spoke a foreign language, although her beauty and their hiking clothes would make them stand out in his memory.

He picked out an apartment building to stop in front of, paid the driver, and tipped him with a dollar bill. Then he and Anana climbed the steps and went into the lobby, which was empty. Waiting until they were sure the cab would be out of sight, they walked back to Wilshire. Here they took a bus.

After several minutes, Kickaha led Anana off the bus and she said, 'What now?' although she did not seem to be too interested at the moment in their next move. She was looking at the gas station across the street. Its architecture was new to Kickaha also. He could compare it only to something out of the Flash Gordon serials. Anana, of course, had seen many different styles. A woman didn't live ten thousand years and in several different universes without seeing a great variety of styles in buildings. But this Earth was such a hodgepodge.

Kickaha told her what he planned next. They would go toward Hollywood and look for a motel or hotel in the cheaper districts. He had learned from a magazine and from newspapers that that area contained many transients – hippies, they called them now – and the wilder younger element. Their clothing and lack of baggage would not cause curiosity.

They caught a cab in two minutes, and it carried them to Sunset Boulevard. Then they walked for quite a while. The sun went down; the lights came on over the city. Sunset Boulevard began to fill up with cars bumper to bumper.

The sidewalks were beginning to be crowded, mainly with the 'hippies' he'd read about. There were also a number of 'characters', which was to be expected in Hollywood.

They stopped and asked some of the aimlessly wandering youths about lodging. A young fellow with shoulder-length hair and a thick 1890 moustache and sideburns, but dressed in expensive looking clothes, gave them some sound information. He wanted to talk some more and even invited them to have dinner with him. It was evident that he was fascinated by Anana, not Kickaha.

Kickaha said to him, 'We'll see you around,' and they left. A half hour later, they were inside their room in a motel on a side street. The room was not plush, but it was more than adequate for Kickaha, who had spent most of the past twenty-four years in primitive conditions. It was not as quiet as he wished, since a party was going on in the next room. A radio or record player was blasting out one of the more screechy examples of Rock, many feet stomped, and many voices shrieked.

While Anana took a shower, he studied the contents of the wallets he'd taken from the two men. Frederic James Mazarin and Jeffrey Velazquez Ramos, according to their drivers' licences, lived on Wilshire Boulevard. His map showed him that the address was close to the termination of Wilshire downtown. He suspected that the two lived in a hotel. Mazarin was forty-eight and Ramos was forty-six. The rest of the contents of the wallets were credit cards (almost unknown in 1946, if he remembered correctly), a few pictures of the two with women, a photo of a woman who might have been Ramos' mother, (three hundred and twenty dollars,) and a slip of paper in Mazarin's wallet with ten initials in one column and telephone numbers in others.

Kickaha went into the bathroom and opened the shower door. He told Anana that he was going across the street to the public telephone booth.

"Why don't you use the telephone here?'

'It goes through the motel switchboard,' he said. 'I just don't want to take any chances of being traced or tapped.'

He walked several blocks to a drug store where he got change. He stood for a moment, considering using the drug store phones and then decided to go back to the booth near the motel. That way, he could watch the motel front while making his calls.

He stopped for a moment by the paperback rack. It had been so long since he'd read a book. Well, he had read the Tishquetmoac books, but they didn't publish anything but science and history and theology. The people of the tier called Atlantis had published fiction, but he had spent very little time among them, although he had planned to do so someday. There had been some books in the Semitic civilization of Khamshem and the Germanic civilization of Dracheland, but the number of novels was very small and the variety was limited. Wolff's palace had contained a library of twenty million books – or recordings of books – but Kickaha had not spent enough time there to read very many.

He looked over the selection, aware that he shouldn't be taking the time to do so, and finally picked three. One was a Tom Wolfe book (but not the Thomas Wolfe he had known), which looked as if it would give him information about the zeitgeist of modern times. One was a factual book by Asimov (who was, it seemed, the same man as the science-fiction writer he remembered), and a book on the black revolution. He went to the magazine counter and purchased *Look, Life, The Saturday Review, The New Yorker*, the *Los Angeles* magazine, and a number of science-fiction magazines.

With his books, magazines, and an evening *Times*, he walked back to the telephone booth. He called Anana first to make sure that she was all right. Then he took pencil and paper and dialled each of the numbers on the slip of paper he had found in Mazarin's wallet.

Three of them were women who disclaimed any knowledge of Mazarin. Three of the numbers did not reply. Kickaha marked these for late calls. One might have been a bookie joint, judging from the talking in the background. The man who answered was as noncommittal as the women. The eighth call got a bartender. Kickaha said he was looking for Mazarin.

The bartender said, 'Ain't you heard, friend? Mazarin was killed today!'

'Somebody *killed* him?' Kickaha said, as if he were shocked. 'Who done it?'

'Nobody knows. The guy was riding with Fred and some of the boys, and all of a sudden the guy pulls Charley's gun out of his pocket, shoots Fred in the chest with it, and takes off, but only after he knocks out Charley, Ramos, and Ziggy.'

'Yeah?' Kickaha said. 'Them guys was pros, too. They must've got careless or something. Say, ain't that gonna makes their boss mad? He must be jumping up and down!'

'You kiddin', friend? Nothin' makes Cambring jump up and down. Look, I gotta go, a customer. Drop around, buy me a drink, I'll fill you in on the gory details.'

Kickaha wrote the name Cambring down and then looked through the phone book. There was no Cambring in the Los Angeles directory or any of the surrounding cities.

The ninth phone number was that of a Culver City garage. The man who answered said he'd never heard of Mazarin. Kickaha doubted that that was true, but there was nothing he could do about it.

The last number was opposite the letters *R. C.* Kickaha hoped that these stood for R. R. Cambring. But the woman who answered was Roma Chalmers. She was as guarded as the others in her replies to his questions.

He called Anana again to make doubly sure that she was all right. Then he returned to the room, where he ordered a meal from the Chicken Delight. He ate everything in the box, but the food had that taste of something disagreeable and of something missing. Anana also ate all of hers but complained.

'Tomorrow's Saturday,' he said. 'If we haven't found any promising leads, we'll go out and get some clothes.'

He took a shower and got dried just before a bottle of Wild Turkey and six bottles of Tuborg were delivered. Anana tried both and settled for the Danish beer. Kickaha sipped a little of the bourbon and made a wry face. The liquor store owner had said that the bourbon was the best in the world. It had been too long since he had tasted whisky; he would have to learn to like it all over again. If he had time, that is, which he doubted. He decided to drink a bottle or two of the Tuborg, which he found tasty, probably because beer-making was well known on the World of Tiers and he had not gotten out of the habit of drinking it.

He sat in a chair and sipped while he slowly read out loud in English from the newspaper to Anana. Primarily, he was looking for any news about Wolff, Jadawin, or the Beller. He sat up straight when he came across an item about Lucifer's Louts. These had been discovered, half naked, beaten up, and burned, on the road out of Lake Arrowhead. The story they gave police was that a rival gang had jumped them.

A page later, he found a story about the crash of a helicopter near Lake Arrowhead. The helicopter, out of the Santa Monica airport, was owned by a Mister Cambring, who had once been put on trial, but not convicted, for bribery of city officials in connection with a land deal. Kickaha whooped with delight and then explained to Anana what a break this was.

The news story did not give Cambring's address. Kickaha called the office of Top Hat Enterprises, which Cambring owned. The phone rang for a long time, and he finally gave up. He then called the *Los Angeles Times* and, after a series of transfers from one person and department to another, some of them involving waits of three or four minutes, he got his information. Mr. Roy Arndell Cambring lived on Rimpau Boulevard. A check of the city map showed that the house was several blocks north of Wilshire.

'This helps,' he said. 'I would have located Cambring if I had to hire a private eye to find him. But that would have taken time. Let's get to bed. We have a lot to do tomorrow.'

However, it was an hour before they fell asleep. Anana wanted to lie quietly in his arms while she talked of this and that, about her life before she had met Kickaha but mostly of incidents after she had met him. Actually, they had not known each other more than two months and their life together had been hectic. But she claimed to be in love with Kickaha and acted as if she were. He loved her but had had enough experience with the Lords to wonder how deep a capacity for love anybody ten thousand years old could possess. It was true, though, that some of the Lords could live for the moment far more intensely than anybody he had ever met simply because a man who lived in eternity had to eat up every moment as if it were his last. He could not bear to think about the unending years ahead.

In the meantime, he was happy with her, although he would have been happier if he could have some leisure and peace so he could get to know her better. Which was exactly what she was complaining about. She did not complain too much. She knew that every situation ended sooner or later.

He fell asleep thinking about this. Sometime in the night, he awoke with a jerk. For a second, he thought somebody must be in the room, and he slid out the knife that lay sheathless by his side under the sheet covering him. His eyes adjusted to the darkness, which was not too deep because of the light through the blinds from the bright neon lights outside and the street lamps. He could see no one.

Slowly, so the bed would not creak, he got out and moved cautiously around the room, the bathroom, and then the closet. The windows were still locked on the inside, the door was locked, and the bureau he had shoved against it had not moved. Nor was there anyone under the bed.

He decided that he had been sleeping on a tightwire too long. He expected, even if unconsciously, to fall off.

There must be more to it than that, however. Something working deep inside him had awakened him. He had been dreaming just before he awoke. Of what?

He could not get his hook into it and bring it up out of the unconscious, though he cast many times. He paced back and forth, the knife still in his hand, and tried to re-create the moment just before awakening. After a while he gave up. But he could not sleep when he lay back down again. He rose again, dressed, and then woke Anana up gently. At his tender touch on her face, she came up off the bed, knife in hand.

He had wisely stepped back. He said, 'It's all right, lover, I just wanted to tell you that I'm leaving to check out Cambring's house. I can't sleep anymore; I feel as if I have something important to do. I've had this feeling before and it's always paid off.'

He did not add that it had sometimes paid off with grave, almost fatal, trouble.

'I'll go with you.'

'No, that won't be necessary. I appreciate your offer, but you stay here and sleep. I promise I won't do anything except scout around it, at a safe distance. You won't have anything to worry about.'

'All right,' she said, half-drowsily. She had full confidence in his abilities. 'Kiss me good night again and get on with you. I'm glad I'm not a restless soul.'

The lobby was empty. There were no pedestrians outside the motel, although a few cars whizzed by. The droning roar of a jet lowering for International Airport seemed to be directly overhead, but its lights placed it quite a few miles southeastward. He trotted on down the street towards the south and hoped that no cops would cruise by. He understood from what he'd read that a man running was suspect anywhere in the city and a man walking at night in the more prosperous districts was also suspect.

He could have taken a taxi to a place near his destination, but he preferred to run. He needed the exercise; if he continued life in this city long, he would be getting soft rapidly.

The smog seemed to have disappeared with the sun. At least, his eyes did not burn and run, although he did get short-winded after having trotted only eight blocks. There must be poisonous oxides hanging invisibly in the air. Or he was deteriorating faster than he had thought possible.

By the map, the Cambring house lay about three and

one-half miles from the motel, not as the crow flies but as a ground-bound human must go.

Once on Rimpau he was in a neighbourhood of fairly old mansions. The neighbourhood looked as if only rich people had lived here, but it was changing. Some of the grounds and houses had deteriorated, and some had been made into apartment dwellings. But a number were still very well kept up.

The Cambring house was a huge three-storey wooden house which looked as if it had been built circa 1920 by someone nostalgic for the architecture popular among the wealthy of the Midwest. It was set up on a high terrace with a walk in the middle of the lawn and a horseshoe-shaped curving driveway. Three cars were parked in the driveway. There were a dozen great oaks and several sycamores on the front lawn and many high bushes, beautifully trimmed, set in among the trees. A high brick wall enclosed all but the front part of the property.

There were lights behind closed curtains in the first and second storeys. There was also a light in the second storey of the garage, which he could partially see. He walked on past the front of the house to the corner. The brick wall ran along the sidewalk here. Part way down the block was another driveway which led to the garage. He stopped before the closed iron gates, which were locked on the inside.

It was possible that there were electronic detecting devices set on the grounds among the trees, but he would have to chance them. Also, it would be well to find out now.

He doubted that this house was lived in by Red Orc. Cambring must be one of Orc's underlings, probably far down in the hierarchy. The Lord of Earth would be ensconced in a truly luxurious dwelling and behind walls which would guard him well.

He set his ring for flesh-piercing powers at up to two hundred feet and placed his knife between his teeth. Instead of returning to the front, he went over the wall on the side of the house. It was more difficult to enter here, but there was better cover.

He backed up into the street and then ran forward, bounded across the sidewalk, and leaped upward. His fingers caught the edge of the wall and he easily pulled himself up and over onto the top of the wall. He lay stretched out on it, watching the house and garage for signs of activity. About four minutes passed. A car, travelling fast, swung around the corner two blocks away and sped down the street. It was possible that the occupants of the house might see him in the beams. He swung on over and dropped onto soft grassy ground behind an oak tree. If he had wished, he could have jumped to the nearest branch, which had been sawed off close to the wall, and descended by the tree. He noted it as a means of escape.

It was now about three in the morning, if his sense of time was good. He had no watch but meant to get one, since he was now in a world where the precise measurement of time was important.

The next ten minutes he spent in quietly exploring the area immediately outside the house and the garage. Three times he went up into a tree to try to look through windows but he could see nothing. He poked around the cars but did not try to open their doors because he thought that they might have alarms. It seemed likely that a gangster like Cambring would be more worried about a bomb being placed in his car than he would about an invasion of his house. The big black Lincoln was not there. He assumed it had been impounded by the police as evidence in the murder. He read the licence numbers several times to memorize them, even though he had a pencil and a piece of paper. During his years in the universe next door, he had been forced to rely on his memory. He had developed it to a power that he would have thought incredible twenty-five years ago. Illiteracy had its uses. How many educated men on Earth could recall the exact topography of a hundred places or draw a map of a five-thousand-mile route or recite a three-thousand-line epic?

In fifteen minutes he had checked out everything he could on the outside and knew exactly where things were in relation to each other. Now was the time to leave. He wished he had not promised Anana that he would only observe the exterior. The temptation to get inside was almost overwhelming. If he could get hold of Cambring and force some information from him . . . but he had promised. And she had gone back to sleep because she trusted him to keep his word. That in itself indicated how much she loved him, because if there was one thing a Lord lacked, it was trust in others.

He crouched for a while behind a bush in the side yard, knowing that he should leave but also knowing that he was hoping something would happen which would force him to take action. Minutes passed.

Then he heard a phone ringing inside the house. A light went on in a second-storey window behind a curtain. He rose and approached the house and applied a small bell-like device to the side of the house. A cord ran from it to a plug, which he stuck in one ear. Suddenly, a man said, 'Yes, sir. I got you. But how did you find them, if I may ask?'

There was a short silence, then the man said, 'I'm sorry, sir. I didn't mean to be nosy, of course. Yes, sir, it won't happen again. Yes, sir, I got you the first time. I know exactly what to do. I'll call you when we start the operation, sir. Good night, sir.'

Kickaha's heart beat faster. Cambring could be talking directly to Red Orc. In any event, something important was happening. Something ominous.

He heard footsteps and buzzers ringing. The voice said – presumably over an intercom – 'Get dressed and up here! On the double! We got work to do! Jump!'

He decided what to do. If he heard anything that indicated that they were not going after him, he would wait until they left and then enter the house. Conditions would have changed so much that it would be stupid for him not to take advantage of their absence. Anana would have to understand that.

If he heard anything that indicated that he and Anana were concerned, he would take off for the nearest public phone booth.

He felt in his pocket for change and cursed. He had one

nickel left over from the calls made that previous evening.

Seven minutes later, eight men left by the front door. Kickaha watched them from behind a tree. Four men got into a Mercedes-Benz and four into a Mercury. He could not be sure which was Cambring, because nobody spoke when they left the house. One man did hold the door open for a tall man with a high curly head of hair and a bold sweeping nose. He suspected that that was Cambring. Also he recognized two: the blond youth and Ramos, the driver of the Lincoln. Ramos had a white bandage over his forehead.

The cars drove off, leaving one car in the driveway. There were also people in the house. He had heard one woman sleepily asking Cambring what was wrong, and a man's voice surlily asking why he had to stay behind. He wanted some action. Cambring had curtly told him to shut up. They were under orders never to leave the house unguarded.

The cars had no sooner disappeared than Kickaha was at the front door. It was locked, but a quick shot of energy from the ring cut through the metal. He swung the door inwards slowly, and stepped inside into a room lit only by a light from a stairwell at the far end. When his eyes adjusted, he could see a phone on a table at the far wall. He went to it, lit a match, and by its light, dialled Anana. The phone rang no more than three times before she answered.

He said softly, 'Anana I'm in Cambring's house! He and his gang are on the way to pick us up. You grab your clothes and get out of there, fast, hear! Don't even bother to dress! Put everything in a bag and take off! Dress behind the motel I'll meet you where we arranged. Got it?'

'Wait!' she said. 'Can't you tell me what's happened?'

'No!' he said and softly replaced the receiver on the phone. He had heard footsteps in the hall upstairs and then the creaking caused by a big man descending the steps slowly.

Kickaha reset the ring for stunning power. He needed someone to question, and he doubted that the woman would know as much about operations as this man.

The faint creakings stopped. Kickaha crouched by the foot of the steps and waited. Suddenly, the lights in the great room went on, and a man catapulted outward from behind the wall which had hidden him. He came down off the steps in a leap, whirling as he did so. He held a big automatic, probably a .45, in his right hand. He landed facing Kickaha and then fell backwards, unconscious, his head driven backwards by the impact of the beam. The gun fell from his hand onto the thick rug.

Kickaha heard the woman upstairs saying, 'Walt! What's the matter? Walt? Is anything wrong?'

Kickaha picked up the gun, flicked on the safety, and stuck it in his belt. Then he walked up the steps and got to the head of the stairwell just as the woman did. She opened her mouth to scream, but he clamped his hand over it and held the knife before her eyes. She went limp as if she thought she could placate him by not struggling. She was correct, for the moment, anyway.

She was a tall, very well built blonde, about thirty-five, in a filmy negligee. Her breath stank of whisky. But good whisky.

'You and Cambring and everybody else in this house mean only one thing to me,' he said. 'As a means to getting to the big boss. That's all. I can let you go without a scratch and care nothing about what you do from then on if you don't bother me. Or I can kill you. Here and now. Unless I get the information I want. You understand me?'

She nodded.

He said, 'I'll let you go. But one scream, and I'll rip out your belly. Understand?'

She nodded again. He took his hand away from her mouth. She was pale and trembling.

'Show me a picture of Cambring,' he said.

She turned and led him to her bedroom, where she indicated a photograph on her bureau dresser. It was of the man he had suspected was Cambring. 'Are you his wife?' he said.

She cleared her throat and said, 'Yes.'

'Anybody else in this house besides Walt?'

She said huskily, 'No.'

'Do you know where Cambring went tonight?'

'No,' she said. She cleared her throat again. 'I don't want to know those things.'

'He's gone off to pick up me and my woman for your big boss,' Kickaha said. 'The big boss would undoubtedly kill us, after he'd tortured us to get everything he wanted to know. So I won't have any mercy on anybody connected with him – if they refuse to co-operate.'

'I don't know anything!' she gasped. 'Roy never tells me anything! I don't even know who the big boss is!'

'Who's Cambring's immediate superior?'

'I don't know. Please believe me I don't know! He gets orders from somebody, I'll admit that! But I don't know!'

She was probably telling the truth. So the next thing to do was to rouse Walt and find out what he knew. He did not have much time.

He went downstairs with Cara ahead of him. The man was still unconscious. Kickaha told Cara to get a glass of water from the nearest bathroom. He threw it over Walt's face. Walt recovered a moment later, but he looked too sick to be a threat. He seemed to be on the verge of throwing up. A big black mark was spreading over the skin on his forehead and nose, and his eyes looked a solid red.

The questioning did not last long. The man, whose full name was Walter Erich Vogel, claimed he also did not know who Cambring's boss was. Nor did he even know where Cambring was going. Kickaha believed this, since Cambring had not said anything about the destination. Apparently, he meant to tell his men after they got started. Cambring called his boss now and then but he carried the phone number in his head.

'It's the old Commie cell idea,' Vogel said. 'So you could torture me from now until doomsday and you wouldn't get anything out of me because I don't know anything.'

Kickaha went to the phone again and, while he kept an eye on the two, dialled Anana's number again. He wasn't surprised when Cambring answered.

'Cambring,' he said, 'this is the man you were sent after. Now hear me out because this message is intended for your big boss. You tell him, or whoever relays messages to him that a Black Beller is loose on Earth.'

There was a silence, one of shock, Kickaha hoped, and then Cambring said, 'What? What the hell you talking about? What's a Black Beller?'

'Just tell your boss that a Black Beller got loose from Jadawin's world. The Beller's in this area, or was yesterday, anyway. Remember, a Black Beller. Came here yesterday from Jadawin's world.'

There was another silence and then Cambring said, 'Listen. The boss knows you got away. But he said that if I got a chance to talk to you, you should come on in. The boss won't hurt you. He just wants to talk to you.'

'You might be right,' Kickaha said. 'But I can't afford to take the chance. No, you tell your boss something. You tell him that I'm not out to get him; I'm not a Lord. I just want to find another Lord and his woman, who came to this world to escape from the Black Bellers. In fact, I'll tell you who that Lord is. It's Jadawin. Maybe your boss will remember him. It's Jadawin, who's changed very much. Jadawin isn't interested in challenging your boss; he couldn't care less. All he wants to do is get back to his own world. You tell him that, though I doubt it'll do any good. I'll call your home tomorrow about noon, so you can relay more of what I have to say to your boss. I'll call your home. Your boss might want to be there so he can talk to me directly.'

'What the hell you gibbering about?' Cambring said. He sounded very angry.

'Just tell your boss what I said. He'll understand,' Kickaha said, and he hung up. He was grinning. If there was one thing that scared a Lord, it was a Black Beller.

The sports car was, as he had suspected, hers. She said she would have to go upstairs to get the keys. He said that that was all right, but he and Vogel would go with her. They went into her bedroom, where Kickaha gave Vogel a slight kick in the back of the head with a beam from the ring. He took Vogel's wallet and dragged him into the closet, where he left him snoring. He then demanded money from the woman, and she gave him six hundred dollars in twenties and fifties. It pleased him that he had been able to live off the enemy so far.

To keep her occupied, he tore down some curtains, and set them on fire with a sweep from the ring. She screamed and dashed into the bathroom to get water. A moment later, he was driving the Jaguar off the driveway. Behind him, screams came through the open doorways as she fought the flames.

At a corner a few blocks east from the motel, he flashed his lights twice to alert Anana. A dark figure emerged from between two houses. She approached warily until she recognized him. She threw their packs and the instrument case into the back seat, got in and said, 'Where did you get this vehicle?'

'Took it from Cambring.' He chuckled and said, 'I left a message with Cambring for Red Orc. Told him that a Black Beller was loose. That ought to divert him. It might even scare him into offering an armistice.'

'Not Red Orc,' she said. 'Not unless he's changed. Which is possible. I did. My brother Luvah did. And you say Jadawin did.'

He told her about his idea for contacting Wolff. 'I should have thought of it sooner, but we have been occupied. And, besides, I've forgotten a lot about Earth.'

For the moment, they would look for new lodgings. However, he was not so sure that they could feel safe even there. It was remarkable that they had been located. Red Orc must have set into action a very large organization to have found them.

'How could he do that?' she said.

'For all I know, his men called every hotel and motel in the Los Angeles area. That would be such a tremendous job, though, I doubt they could have gone through more than a small percentage of them. Maybe they were making random spot calls. Or maybe they were going through them all, one by one, and were lucky.'

'If that is so, then we won't be safe when we check in at the next place.'

'I just don't believe that even the Lord of the Earth would have an organization big enough to check out all the motels and hotels in so short a time,' he said. 'But we'll leave the area, go to the Valley, as they so quaintly call it here.'

When they found a motel in Laurel Canyon, he ran into difficulties.

The clerk wanted his driver's licence and the licence number of his car. Kickaha did not want to give him the licence number, but, since the clerk showed no signs of checking up on him, Kickaha gave him a number made up in his head. He then showed him Ramos' driver's licence. The clerk copied down the number and looked once at the photograph. Ramos had a square face with a big beaky nose, black eyes, and a shock of black hair. Despite this, the clerk did not seem to notice.

Kickaha, however, was suspicious. The fellow was too smooth. Perhaps he did not really care whether or not Kickaha was the person he claimed to be, but then, again, he might. Kickaha said nothing, took the keys, and led Anana out of the lobby. Instead of going to their room on the second floor, he stood outside the door, where he could not be seen. A minute later, he heard the clerk talking to somebody. He looked in. The clerk was sitting at the switchboard with his back to the door. Kickaha tiptoed in closer.

'. . . not his,' the clerk was saying. 'Yeah, I checked out the licence, soon as they left. The car's parked near here. Listen, you . . .'

He stopped because he had turned his head and had seen Kickaha. He turned it away, slowly, and said, 'OK. See you.'

He took off the earphones and stood up and said, smiling, 'May I help you?'

'We decided to eat before we went to bed; we haven't eaten all day,' Kickaha said, also smiling. 'Where's the nearest good restaurant?'

The clerk spoke slowly, as if he were trying to think of one that would suit them. Kickaha said, 'We're not particular. Any place'll do.'

A moment later, he and Anana drove off. The clerk stood in the front door and watched them. He had seen them put their packs and the case in the car, so he probably did not believe that they were coming back.

He was thinking that they could sleep in the car tonight, provided the police weren't looking for it. Tomorrow they would have to buy clothes and a suitcase or two. He would have to get rid of this car, but the problem of renting or buying a car without the proper papers was a big one.

He pulled into a service station and told the attendant to fill her up. The youth was talkative and curious; he wanted to know where they'd been, up in the mountains? He liked hiking, too.

Kickaha made up a story. He and his wife had been bumming around but decided to come down and dig L.A. They didn't have much money; they were thinking about selling the car and getting a second-hand VW. They wanted to stay the night some place where they didn't ask questions if the colour of your money was right.

The attendant told them of a motel near Tarzana in Van Nuys which fitted all Kickaha's specifications. He grinned and winked at them, sure they were engaged in something illegal (or rebellious) and wished them luck. Maybe he could get them a good bargain on the Jag.

A half hour later, he and Anana fell into a motel bed and were asleep at once.

He got up at ten. Anana was sleeping soundly. After shaving and showering, he woke her long enough to tell her what he planned. He went across the street to a restaurant, ate a big breakfast, bought a paper, and then returned to the room. Anana was still sleeping. He called the *Los Angeles Times* ad department and dictated an item for the personal column. He gave as his address the motel and also gave a fictitious name. He had thought about using Ramos' name in case the *Times* man checked out the address. But he did not want any tie between the ad and Cambring, if he could help it. He promised to send his cheque immediately, and then, hanging up, forgot about it.

He checked the personals of the morning's *Times.* There were no messages that could be interpreted as being from Wolff.

When Anana woke, he said 'While you're eating breakfast, I'll use a public phone booth to call Cambring,' he said. 'I'm sure he's gotten the word to Red Orc.'

Cambring answered at once as if he had been waiting by the phone. Kickaha said, 'This is your friend of last night, Cambring. Did you pass on my information about the Black Beller?'

Cambring's voice sounded as if he were controlling anger.

'Yes, I did.'

'What did he say?'

'*He* said that he'd like to meet you. Have a conference of war.'

'Where?'

'Wherever you like.'

Good, thought Kickaha. *He doesn't think I'm so dumb that I'd walk into his parlour. But he's confident that he can set up a trap no matter where I meet him. If, that is, he himself shows up. I doubt that. He'd be far too cagy for that. But he'll have to send someone to represent him, and that someone might be higher up than Cambring and a step closer to the Lord.*

'I'll tell you where we'll meet in half an hour,' Kickaha said. 'But, before I hang up, did your boss have anything else to say I should hear?'

'No.'

Kickaha clicked the phone down. He found Anana in a booth in the restaurant. He sat down and said, 'I don't know whether Orc's got hold of Wolff or not. I don't even know for sure whether Cambring repeated my message about Wolff and Chryseis, but Orc knows the gate was activated twice before we came through and that one of the people coming through was a Black Beller. I don't think he's got Wolff and Chryseis, because if he did, he'd use them as a way to trap me. He'd know I'd be galloping in to save them.'

'Perhaps,' she said. 'But he may feel that he doesn't have to let you know he has Wolff and Chryseis. He may feel confident that he can catch us without saying anything about them. Or perhaps he's withholding his knowledge until a more suitable time.'

'You Lords sure figure out the angles,' he said. 'As suspicious a lot as the stars have ever looked down on.'

'Look who's talking' she said in English.

They returned to their room, picked up their bags and the case, and went to the car. They drove off without checking out, since Kickaha did not think it wise to let anybody know what they were doing if it could be helped. In Tarzana, he went into a department store and checked out clothes for himself and Anana. This took an hour, but he did not mind keeping Cambring waiting. Let him and his boss sweat for a while.

While he was waiting for his trousers to be altered, he made the call. Again, Cambring answered immediately.

'Here's what we'll do,' Kickaha said. 'I'll be at a place fairly close to your house. I'll call you when I get there, and I'll give you twelve minutes to get to our meeting place. If you aren't there by then, I move on. Or if it looks like a trap, I'll take off, and that'll be the last you'll see of me – at a meeting place, that is. Your boss can take care of the Beller himself.'

'What the hell is this Beller you're talking about?' Cambring said angrily.

'Ask your boss,' Kickaha said, knowing that Cambring would not dare do this. 'Look, I'm going to be in a place where I can see on all sides. I want just two men to meet me. You, because I know you, and your boss. You'll advance no closer than sixty yards, and your boss will then come ahead. Got it? So long!'

At noon, after eating half a hamburger and a glass of milk, he called Cambring. He was at a restaurant only a few blocks from the meeting place. Cambring answered again before the phone had finished its third ring. Kickaha told him where he was to meet him and under what conditions.

'Remember,' he said. 'If I smell anything fishy, I take off like an Easter bunny with birth pangs.'

He hung up. He and Anana drove as quickly as traffic would permit. His destination was the Los Angeles County Art Museum. Kickaha parked the car around the corner and put the keys under the floor mat, in case only one of them could get back to it. They proceeded on foot behind the museum and walked through the parking lot.

Anana had dropped behind him so that anyone watching would not know she was with Kickaha. Her long glossy black hair was coiled up into a Psyche knot, and she wore a white low-cut frilly blouse and very tight green-and-red striped culottes. Dark glasses covered her eyes, and she carried an artist's sketch pad and pencils. She also carried a big leather purse which contained a number of items that would have startled any scientifically knowledgeable Earthling.

While Kickaha hailed down a cab, she walked slowly across the grass. Kickaha gave the cab driver a twenty-dollar bill as evidence of his good intentions and of the tip to come. He told him to wait in the parking lot, motor running, ready to take off when Kickaha gave the word. The cab driver raised his eyebrows and said, 'You aren't planning on robbing the museum?'

'I'm planning on nothing illegal,' Kickaha said. 'Call me eccentric. I just like to leave in a hurry sometimes.'

'If there's any shooting, I'm taking off,' the driver said. 'With or without you. And I'm reporting to the cops. Just so you know, see?'

Kickaha liked to have more than one avenue of escape. If Cambring's men should be cruising around the neighbourhood, they might spot their stolen car and set a trap for Kickaha. In fact, he was betting that they would. But if the way to the cab was blocked, and he had to take the route to the car, and that wasn't blocked, he would use the car.

However, he felt that the driver was untrustworthy, not that he blamed him for feeling suspicious.

He added a ten to the twenty and said, 'Call the cops now, if you want. I don't care, I'm clean.'

Hoping that the cabbie wouldn't take him up he turned and strode across the cement of the parking lot and then across the grass to the tar pit. Anana was sitting down on a concrete bench and sketching the mammoth which seemed to be sinking into the black liquid. She was an excellent artist, so that anybody who looked over her shoulder would see that she knew her business.

Kickaha wore dark glasses, a purple sleeveless and neckless shirt, a big leather belt with fancy silver buckle, and levis. Under his long red hair, against the bone behind his ear, was a receiver. The device he wore on his wrist contained an audio transmitter and a beamer six times as powerful as that in his ring.

Kickaha took his station at the other end of the tar pit. He stood near the fence beyond which was the statue of a huge prehistoric bear. There were about fifty people scattered here and there, none of whom looked as if they would be Cambring's men. This, of course, meant nothing.

A minute later, he saw a large grey Rolls-Royce swing into the parking lot. Two men got out and crossed the grass in a straight line towards him. One was Ramos. The other was tall and gangly and wore a business suit, dark glasses, and a hat. When he came closer, Kickaha saw a horse-faced man of about fifty. Kickaha doubted then that he would be Red Orc, because no Lord, not even if he were twenty thousand years old, looked as if he were over thirty.

Anana's voice sounded in his ear. 'It's not Red Orc.'

He looked around again. There were two men on his left, standing near the fountain by the museum and two men on his right, about twenty yards beyond Anana. They could be Cambring's men.

His heart beat faster. The back of his neck felt chilled. He looked through the fence across the pit at Wilshire Boulevard. Parking was forbidden there at any time. But a car was there, its hood up and a man looking under it. A man sat in the front seat and another in the rear.

'He's going to try to grab me,' Kickaha said. 'I've spotted seven of his men, I think.'

'Do you want to abandon your plan?' she said.

'If I do, you know the word,' he said. 'Watch it! Here they come!'

Ramos and the gangly man stopped before him. The gangly man said, 'Paul?' using the name Kickaha had given Cambring.

Kickaha nodded. He saw another big car enter the parking lot. It was too far for him to distinguish features, but the driver, wearing a hat and dark glasses, could be Cambring. There were three others in his car.

'Are you Red Orc?' Kickaha said, knowing that the tall man was probably carrying a device which would transmit the conversation to the Lord, wherever he was.

'Who? Who's Redark?' the tall man said. 'My name is Kleist. Now, Mr. Paul, would you mind telling me what you want.'

Kickaha spoke in the language of the Lords, 'Red Orc! I am not a Lord but an Earthling who found a gate to the universe of Jadawin, whom you may remember. I came back to Earth, though I did not want to, to hunt down the Beller. I have no desire to stay here; I wish only to kill the Beller and get back to my adopted world. I have no interest in challenging you.'

Kleist said, 'What the hell you gibbering about? Speak English, man!'

Ramos looked uneasy. He said, 'He's flipped.'

Kleist suddenly looked dumbfounded. Kickaha guessed that he was getting orders.

'Mr. Paul,' Kleist said, 'I am empowered to offer you complete amnesty. Just come with us and we will introduce you to the man you want to see.'

'Nothing doing,' Kickaha said. 'I'll work with your boss, but I won't put myself in his power. He may be all right, but I have no reason to trust him. I would like to cooperate with him, however, in tracking down the Beller.'

Kleist's expression showed that he did not understand the reference to the Beller.

Kickaha looked around again. The men on his left and right were drifting closer. The two men in the car on Wilshire had gotten out. One was looking under the hood with the other man, but the third was gazing through the fence at Kickaha. When he saw Kickaha looking at him, he slowly turned away.

Kickaha said angrily, 'You were told that only two of you should come! You're trying to spring a trap on me! You surely don't think you can kidnap me here in the middle of all these people?'

'Now, now, Mr. Paul!' Kleist said. 'You're mistaken! Don't be nervous! There's only two of us, and we're here to talk to you, only that.'

Anana said, 'A police car has just pulled up behind that car on the street.'

Kleist and Ramos looked at each other; it was evident that they had also seen the police car. But they looked as if they had no intention of leaving.

Kickaha said, 'If your boss would like me to help, he'll have to think of some way of guaranteeing me passage back.'

He decided he might as well spring his surprise now. The Lord knew that there was a woman with Kickaha, and while he had no way of knowing that she was a Lord, he must suspect it. Kickaha had only been on Earth a short time when the Lord's men had seen her with him. And since he knew that the gate had been activated twice before Kickaha came along, he must suspect that the other party – or parties – was also a Lord.

Now was the time to tell Red Orc about them. This would strengthen Kickaha's bargaining position and it might stop the effort to take him prisoner now.

'You tell your boss,' he said, 'that there are four other Lords now on Earth.'

Kickaha was not backward about exaggerating if it might confuse or upset the enemy. There might come a time when he could use the two nonexistent Lords as leverage.

'Also,' he added, 'there are two Earthlings who have come from Jadawin's world. Myself and a woman who is with Jadawin.'

That ought to rock him, he thought. Arouse his curiosity even more. He must be wondering how two Earthlings got into Jadawin's world in the first place and how they got back here.

'You tell your boss,' Kickaha said, 'that none of us, except for the Beller, mean him any harm. We just want to kill the Beller and get the hell out of this stinking universe.'

Kickaha thought that Red Orc should be able to understand that. What Lord in his right mind would want to take control of Earth from another Lord? What Lord would want to stay here when he could go to a much nicer, if much smaller, universe?

Kleist was silent for a moment. His head was slightly cocked as if he were listening to an invisible demon on his shoulder. Then he said, 'What difference does it make if there are four Lords?'

It was obvious that Kleist was relaying the message and that he did not understand the references.

Kickaha spoke in the language of the Lords. 'Red Orc! You have forgotten the device that every Lord carries in his brain. The alarm that rings in every Lord's head when he gets close to the metal bell of a Beller! With four Lords searching for the Beller, the chances for finding him are greater!'

Kleist had dropped any pretence that he was not in direct communication with his chief. He said, 'How does he know that *you* are not a Beller?'

'If I were a Beller, why would I get into contact with you, let you know you had a dangerous enemy loose in your world?'

'He says,' Kleist reported, his face becoming blanker as he talked, as if he were turning into a mechanical transceiver, 'that a Beller would try to locate all Lords as quickly as possible. After all, a Lord is the only one besides a Beller who knows that Bellers exist. Or who can do anything about them. So you would try to find him, just as you are now doing. Even if it meant your life. Bellers are notorious for sacrificing one of their number if they can gain an advantage thereby.

'He also says, how does he know that these so-called Lords are not your fellow Bellers?'

Kickaha spoke in the Lords' tongue. 'Red Orc! You are trying my patience. I have appealed to you because I know of your vast resources! You haven't got much choice, Red Orc! If you force me to cut off contact with you, then you won't know that I'm not a Beller and your sleep will be hideous with nightmares about the Bellers at large! In fact, the only way you can be sure that I'm not a Beller is to work with me, but under my terms! I insist on that!'

The only way to impress a Lord was to be even more arrogant than he.

Anana's voice said, 'The car's gone. The police must have scared them out. The police car's going now.'

Kickaha raised his arm and muttered into the transceiver, 'Where are the others?'

'Closing in. They're standing by the fence and pretending to look at the statues. But they're working towards you.'

He looked at Kleist and Ramos across the grass. The two cars he had suspected were now empty, except for one man, whom he thought would be Cambring. The others were among the picnickers on the grass. He saw two men who looked grim and determined and tough; they could be Cambring's.

'We'll take off to my left,' he said. 'Around the fence and across Wilshire. If they follow us, it'll have to be on foot. At first, at least.'

He flicked a look towards Anana. She had gotten up from the bench and was strolling towards him.

Kleist said, 'Very well. I am authorized to accept your terms.'

He smiled disarmingly and stepped closer. Ramos tensed.

'Couldn't we go elsewhere? It's difficult to carry on a conversation here. But it'll be wherever you say.'

Kickaha was disgusted. He had just been about to agree that it would be best to tie in with Red Orc. Through him, the Beller and Wolff and Chryseis might be found, and after that the dam could break and the devil take the hindmost. But the Lord was following the bent of his kind; he was trusting his power, his ability to get anything or anybody he wanted.

Kickaha made one last try. 'Hold it! Not a step closer! You ask your boss if he remembers Anana, his niece, or Jadawin, his nephew? Remembers how they looked? If he can identify them, then he'll know I'm telling the truth.'

Kleist was silent and then nodded his head. He said, 'Of course. My boss agrees. Just let him have a chance to see them.'

It was no use. Kickaha knew then what Red Orc was thinking. It should have occurred to Kickaha. The brains of Anana and Wolff could be housing the minds of the Bellers.

Kleist, still smiling, reached into his jacket slowly, so that Kickaha would not be thinking he was reaching for a gun. He brought out a pen and pad of paper and said, 'I'll write down this number for you to call, and . . .'

Not for a second did Kickaha believe that the pen was only a pen. Evidently Orc had entrusted Kleist with a beamer. Kleist did not know it, but he was doomed. He had heard too much during the conversation, and he knew about a device which should not be existing on Earth as yet.

There was no time to tell Kleist that in the hope that he could be persuaded to desert the Lord.

Kickaha leaped to one side just as Kleist pointed the pen at him. Kickaha was quick, but he was touched by the beam on the shoulder and hurled sideways to the ground. He rolled on, seeing Kleist throw his hands up into the air, the pen flying away, and then Kleist staggered back one step and fell onto his back. Kickaha leaped up and dived towards the pen, even though his left shoulder and arm felt as if a two-by-four had slammed into it. Ramos, however, made no effort to grab the pen. Probably, he did not know what it really was.

Women were shrieking and men were yelling, and there was much running around.

When he got to his feet, he saw why. Kleist and three of his men were unconscious on the ground. Six men were running towards them – these must have been the latecomers – and were shoving people out of their way.

The fourth man who had been sneaking up on him was pulling a gun from an underarm holster.

Ramos, seeing this, shouted, 'No! No guns! You know that!'

Kickaha aimed the beamer-pen, which, fortunately, was activated by pressing a slide, not by code words, and the man seemed to fold up and be lifted off the ground. He sailed back, hit on his buttocks, straightened out, and lay still, arms outspread, his face grey. The gun lay on the ground several feet before him.

Kickaha turned and saw Anana running towards him. She had shot a beam at the same time that Kickaha shot his, and the gunman had gotten a double impact.

Kickaha leaped forward, scooped up the gun, and hurled it over the fence into the tar pit. He and Anana ran around the fence and up the slope onto the sidewalk. There was no crosswalk here, and the traffic was heavy. But it was also slow because the traffic light a half block away was red.

The two ran between the cars, forcing them to slam on their brakes. Horns blatted, and several people yelled at them out the windows.

Once they reached the other side, they looked behind them. The traffic had started up again, and the seven men after them were, for the moment, helpless.

'Things didn't work out right,' Kickaha said. 'I was hoping that I could grab Kleist and get away with him. He might've been the lead to Red Orc.'

Anana laughed, though a little nervously. 'Nobody can accuse you of being underconfident,' she said. 'What now,'

'The cops'll be here pretty quick,' he said. 'Yeah, look,

Cambring's men are all going back. I bet they got orders to get Kleist and the others out before the cops get here.'

He grabbed Anana's hand and began running east towards the corner. She said, 'What're you doing?'

'We'll cross back at the traffic light while they're busy and then run like hell down Curson Street. Cambring's there!'

She did not ask any more. But to get away from the enemy and then to run right back into his mouth seemed suicidal.

The two were now opposite the men about a hundred yards away. Kickaha looked between the trees lining the street and saw the unwounded men supporting Kleist and three others. In the distance, a siren wailed. From the way Cambring's men hurried, they had no doubt that it was coming after them.

Cambring, locking anxious, was standing by the car. He stiffened when he felt the pen touch his back and heard Kickaha's voice.

Cambring did not look around but got into the front seat as directed. Anana and Kickaha got into the rear seat, and ducked down. Kickaha kept the pen jammed against Cambring's back.

Cambring protested once. 'You can't get away with this! You're crazy!'

'Just shut up!' Kickaha said.

Thirty seconds later, Kleist, supported by two men, reached the car. Kickaha swung out the back door and pointed the pen at them, saying, 'Put Kleist into the front seat.'

The two holding Kleist halted. The others, forming a rear guard, reached for their guns, but Kickaha shouted, 'I'll kill Kleist and Cambring both. And you, too, with this!'

He waved the pen. The others knew by now that the pen was a weapon of some sort even if they did not know its exact nature. They seemed to fear it more than a gun, probably because its nature was in doubt.

They stopped. Kickaha said, 'I'm taking these two! The

cops'll be here in a minute! You better take off, look out for yourselves!'

The two holding Kleist carried him forward and shoved him into the front seat. Cambring had to push against Kleist to keep him from falling on him like a sack full of garbage. Kickaha quickly got out of the car and went around to get into the driver's seat, while Anana held the pen on the others.

He started the motor, backed up with a screech of tyres, jerked it to a stop, turned, and roared out of the parking lot. The car went up and down violently as they jumped the dip between the lot entrance and the street. Kickaha shouted to Anana, and she reached over the seat, felt behind Kleist's ear, and came up with the transceiver. It was a metal disc thin as a postage stamp and the size of a dime.

She stuck it behind her ear and also removed Kleist's wristwatch and put it on her own wrist.

He now had Cambring and Kleist. What could he do with them?

Anana suddenly gasped and pushed at Cambring, who had slumped over against Kickaha. In a swift reaction, he had shoved out with his elbow, thinking for a second that Cambring was attacking him. Then he understood that Cambring had fallen against him. He was unconscious.

Another look convinced him that Cambring was dead or close to death. His skin was the grey-blue of a corpse.

Anana said, 'They're both dead'

Kickaha pulled the car over to the kerb and stopped. He pointed frantically at her. She stared a moment, and then saw what he was trying to communicate. She quickly shed the receiver and Kleist's wristwatch as if she had discovered that she was wearing a leper's clothing.

Kickaha reached over and pulled her close to him and whispered in her ear, 'I'll pick up the watch and receiver with a handkerchief and stick them in the trunk until we can get rid of them. I think you'd be able to hear Red Orc's voice now, if you still had that receiver behind your ear. He'd be telling you he'd just killed Cambring and he was going to kill you unless we surrendered to him.'

He picked up Cambring's wrist and with a pencil pried up the watch compartment. There was a slight discolouration under it on the skin. With the pencil, he pried loose the disc from behind Cambring's ear and exposed a brown-blue disc-shaped spot.

Kleist groaned. His eyelids fluttered, and he looked up. Kickaha started the car again and pulled away from the kerb, and then turned north. As they drove slowly in the heavy traffic, Kleist managed to straighten himself. To do this, he had to push Cambring over against Kickaha. Anana gave a savage order, and Kleist got Cambring off the seat and onto the floor. Since the body took up so much space, Kleist had to sit with his knees almost up to his chin.

He groaned again and said, 'You killed him.'

Kickaha explained what had happened. Kleist did not believe him. He said, 'What kind of a fool do you think I am.'

Kickaha grinned and said, 'Very well, so you don't believe in the efficacy of the devices, the workings of which I've just explained to you. I could put them back on you and so prove the truth of what I've told you. You wouldn't know it, because you'd be dead and your boss would've scored one on us.'

He drove on until he saw a sign which indicated a parking lot behind a business building. He drove down the alley and turned into it. The lot was a small one, enclosed on three sides by the building. There were no windows from which he could be seen, and, for the moment, there was no one in the lot or the alley. He parked, then got out and motioned to Kleist to get out. Anana held the pen against his side.

Kickaha dragged Cambring's body out and rolled it under a panel truck. Then they got back into the car and drove off, towards the motel.

Kickaha was worried. He may have pushed Red Orc to the point where he would report the Rolls as stolen. Up to now he had kept the police out of it, but Kickaha did not doubt that the Lord would bring them in if he felt it necessary. The Lord must have great influence, both politically and financially, even if he remained an anonymous figure. With Kickaha and Anana picked up by the police, the Lord could then arrange for his men to seize them. All he had to do was to pay the bail and catch them after they'd gone a few blocks from the police station.

And if Kleist knew anything which might give Kickaha a lead to Red Orc, the Lord might act to make sure that Kleist could not do so.

Kleist, at this moment, was not co-operating. He would not even reply to Kickaha's questions. Finally, he said, 'Save your breath. You'll get nothing from me.'

When they reached the motel, Kleist got out of the car slowly. He looked around as if he would like to run or shout, but Kickaha had warned him that if he tried anything, he would get enough power from the pen to knock his head off. He stepped into the motel room ahead of Kickaha, who did not even wait for Anana to shut the door before stunning his prisoner with a minimum jolt from the pen.

Before he could recover, Kleist had been injected with a serum that Kickaha had brought from Wolff's palace in that other world.

During the next hour, they learned much about the workings and the people of what Kleist referred to as The Group. His immediate boss was a man named Alfredo Roulini. He lived in Beverly Hills, but Kleist had never been in his home. Always, Roulini gave orders over the phone or met Kleist and other underlings at Kleist's or Cambring's home.

Roulini, as described by Kleist, could not be Red Orc.

Kickaha paced back and forth, frowning, running his fingers through his long red hair.

'Red Orc will know, or at least surmise, that we've gotten Roulini's name and address from Kleist. So he'll warn Roulini, and they'll have a trap set for us. He may have been arrogant and overconfident before, but he knows now we're no pushovers. We've given him too hard a time. We won't be able to get near Roulini, and even if we did, I'll bet we'd find out that he has no more idea of the true identity or location of Red Orc than Kleist.'

'That's probably true,' Anana said. 'So the only thing to do is to force Red Orc to come into the open.'

'I'm thinking the same thing,' he said. 'But how do you flush him out?'

Anana exclaimed, 'The Beller!'

Kickaha said, 'So far, we don't know where the Beller is, and, much as I hate to think about it, may never.'

'Don't say that!' she said. 'We have to find him!'

Her determination, he knew, did not originate from concern for the inhabitants of Earth. She was terrified only that the Bellers might one day become powerful enough to gate from Earth into other universes, the pocket worlds owned by the Lords. She was concerned only for herself and, of course, for him. Perhaps for Luvah, the wounded brother left behind to guard Wolff's palace. But she would never be able to sleep easily until she was one hundred per-cent certain that no Bellers were alive in the one thousand and eight known universes.

Nor would Red Orc sleep any more easily.

Kickaha tied Kleist's hands behind him, tied his feet together, and taped his mouth. Anana could not understand why he didn't just kill the man. Kickaha explained, as he had done a number of times, that he would not do so unless he thought it was necessary. Besides, they were in enough trouble without leaving a corpse behind them.

After removing Kleist's wallet, he put him in the closet.

'He can stay there until tomorrow when the cleaning woman comes in. But I think we'll move on. Let's go across the street and eat. We have to put something in our bellies.'

They walked across the street at the corner, and went down half a block to the restaurant. They got a booth by the window, from which he could see the motel.

While they were eating, he told her what his plans were. 'A Lord will come as swiftly for a pseudo-Beller as for the real thing, because he won't know for sure which is which.

We make our own Beller and get some publicity, too, and so make sure that Red Orc finds out about it.'

'There's still a good chance that he won't come personally,' she said.

'How's he going to know whether or not the Beller is for real unless he does show?' he said. 'Or has the Beller brought to him.'

'But you couldn't get out then!' she said.

'Maybe I couldn't get out, but I'm not there yet. We've got to play this by ear. I don't see anything else to do, do you?'

They rose, and he stopped at the register to pay their bill. Anana whispered to him to look through the big plate glass window at the motel. A police car was turning into the motel grounds.

Kickaha watched the two policemen get out and look at the licence plate on the rear of the Rolls. Then one went into the manager's office while the other checked out the Rolls. In a moment, the officer and the manager came out, and all three went into the motel room that Anana and Kickaha had just left.

'They'll find Kleist in the closet,' Kickaha murmured. 'We'll take a taxi back to L.A. and find lodging somewhere else.'

They had the clothes they were wearing, the case with the Horn of Shambarimen, their beamer rings with a number of power charges, the beamer-pen, their ear receivers and wrist chronometer transmitters, and the money they'd taken from Baum, Cambring, and Kleist. The latter had provided another hundred and thirty-five dollars.

They went outside into the heat and the eye-burning, sinus-searing smog. He picked up the morning *Los Angeles Times* from a corner box, and then waited for a taxi. Presently, one came along, and they rode out of the Valley. On the way, he read the personals column, which contained his ad. None of the personals read as if they had been planted by Wolff. The two got out of the taxi, walked two blocks, and took another taxi to a place chosen at random by Kickaha.

They walked around for a while. He got a haircut and purchased a hat and also talked the clerk out of a woman's hat box. At a drugstore, he bought some hair dye and other items, including shaving equipment, toothbrushes and paste, and a nail file. In a pawnshop he bought two suitcases, a knife which had an excellent balance, and a knife-sheath.

Two blocks away, they checked in at a third-rate hotel. The desk clerk seemed interested only in whether they could pay in advance or not. Kickaha, wearing his hat and dark glasses, hoped that the clerk wasn't paying them much attention. Judging from the stink of cheap whisky on his breath he was not very perceptive at the moment.

Anana, looking around their room, said, 'The place we just left was a hovel. But it's a palace compared to this!'

'I've been in worse,' he said. 'Just so the cockroaches aren't big enough to carry us off.'

They spent some time dying their hair. His red-bronze became a dark brown, and her hair, as black and glossy as a Polynesian maiden's, became corn-yellow.

'It's no improvement, but it's a change,' he said. 'So, now to a metalworker's.'

The telephone books had given the addresses of several in this area. They walked to the nearest place advertising metalworking, where Kickaha gave his specifications and produced the money in advance. During his conversation, he had studied the proprietor's character. He concluded that he was open to any deal where the money was high and the risk low.

He decided to cache the Horn. Much as he hated to have it out of his sight, he no longer cared to risk the chance of Red Orc's getting his hands on it. If he had not carried it with him when he left the motel, it would be in the hands of the police by now. And if Orc heard about it, which he was bound to do, Orc would quickly enough have it.

The two went to the Greyhound Bus station, where he put the case and Horn in a locker.

'I gave that guy an extra twenty bucks to do a rush job,' he said. 'He promised to have it ready by five. In the meantime, I propose we rest in the tavern across the street from our palatial lodgings. We'll watch our hotel for any interesting activities.'

The Blue Bottle Fly was a sleazy beer joint, which did, however, have an unoccupied booth by the front window. This was covered by a dark blind, but there was enough space between the slats for Kickaha to see the front of the hotel. He ordered a coke for Anana and a beer for himself. He drank almost none of the beer but every fifteen minutes ordered another one just to keep the management happy. While he watched, he questioned Anana about Red Orc. There was so little that he knew about their enemy.

'He's my *krathlrandroon,*' Anana said. 'My mother's brother. He left the home universe over fifteen thousand Earth years ago to make his own. That was five thousand years before I was born. But we had statues and photos of him, and he came back once when I was about fifteen years old, so I knew how he looked. But I don't remember him now. Despite which, if I were to see him again, I might know him immediately. There is the family resemblance, you know. Very strong. If you should ever see a man who is the male counterpart of me, you will be looking at Red Orc. Except for the hair. His is not black, it is a dark bronze. Like yours. Exactly like yours.

'And now that I come to think of it . . . I wonder why it didn't strike me before . . . you look much like him.'

'Come on now!' Kickaha said. 'That would mean I'd look like you! I deny that!'

'We could be cousins, I think,' she said.

Kickaha laughed, though his face was warm and he felt anxious for some reason.

'Next, you'll be telling me I'm the long-lost son of Red Orc.'

'I don't know that he has any son,' she said thoughtfully. 'But you could be his child, yes.'

'I know who my parents are,' he said. 'Hoosier farm folk. And they knew who their ancestors were, too. My father was of Irish descent – what else, Finnegan, for God's sake? – and my mother was Norwegian and a quarter Catawba Indian.'

'I wasn't trying to prove anything,' she said. 'I was just commenting on certain undeniable resemblances. Now that I think about it, your eyes are that peculiar leaf-green ... yes, exactly like it ... I'd forgotten ... Red Orc's eyes are yours.'

Kickaha put his hand on hers and said, 'Hold it!'

He was looking through the slats. She turned and said, 'A police car!'

'Yeah, double-parked outside the hotel. They're both going in. They could be checking on someone else. So let's not get panicky.'

'Since when did I ever panic?' she said coldly.

'My apologies. That's just my manner of speaking.'

Fifteen minutes passed. Then a car pulled up behind the police car. it contained three men in civilian clothes, two of whom got out and went into the hotel. The car drove away.

Kickaha said, 'Those two looked like plainclothesmen to me.'

The two uniformed policemen came out and drove away. The two suspected detectives did not come out of the hotel for thirty minutes. They walked down to the corner and stood for a minute talking, and then one returned. He did not, however, re-enter the hotel. Instead, he crossed the street.

Kickaha said, 'He's got the same idea we had! Watch the hotel from here!' He stood up and said, 'Come on! Out the back way. Saunter along, but fast!'

The back way was actually a side entrance, which led to a blind alley the open end of which was on the street. The two walked northward towards the metalworking shop.

Kickaha said, 'Either the police got their information from Red Orc or they're checking us out because of Kleist. It doesn't matter. We're on the run, and Orc's got the advantage. As long as he can keep pushing us, we aren't going to get any closer to him. Maybe.'

They had several hours yet before the metalworker

would be finished. Kickaha led Anana into another tavern, much higher class, and they sat down again. He said, 'You just barely got started telling me the story of your uncle.'

'There isn't really much to tell,' she said. 'Red Orc was a figure of terror among the Lords for a long time. He successfully invaded the universes of at least ten Lords and killed them. Then he was badly hurt when he got into the word of Vala, my sister. Red Orc is very wily and a man of many resources and great power. But my sister Vala combines all the qualities of a cobra and a tiger. She hurt him badly, as I said, but in doing she got hurt herself. In fact, she almost died. Red Orc escaped, however, and came back to this universe, which was the first one he made after leaving the home world.'

Kickaha sat up and said, '*What*'

His hand, flailing out, knocked over his glass of beer. He paid it no attention but stared at her.

'What did you say?'

'You want me to repeat the whole thing?'

'No, no! That final . . . the part where you said he came back to *this* universe, the first one he *made!*'

'Yes? What's so upsetting about that?'

Kickaha did not stutter often. But now he could not quite get the words out.

Finally, he said, 'L-listen! I accept the idea of the pocket universes of the Lords, because I've lived in one half my life and I know others exist because I've been told about them by a man who doesn't lie and I've seen the Lords of other universes, including you! And I know there are at least one thousand and eight of these relatively small manufactured universes.

'But I had always thought . . . I still think . . . it's impossible . . . my universe is a natural one, just as you say your home universe, Gardzrintrah, was.'

'I didn't say *that,*' she said softly. She took his hand and squeezed it.

'Dear Kickaha, does it really upset you so much?'

'You must be mistaken, Anana,' he said. 'Do you have any idea of the *vastness* of *this* universe? In fact, it's infinite! No man could *make* this incredibly complex and gigantic world! My God, the nearest star is four and some light-years away and the most distant is billions of light-years away, and there must be others billions of billions of light-years beyond these!

'And then there is the age of this universe! Why, this planet alone is two and one-half billion years old the last I heard! That's a hell of a lot older than fifteen thousand years, when the Lords moved out of their home world to make their pocket universes! A hell of a lot older!'

Anana smiled and patted his hand as if she were his grandmother and he a very small child.

'There, there. No reason to get upset, lover. I wonder why Wolff didn't tell you. Probably he forgot it when he lost his memory. And when he got his memory back, he did not get all of it back. Or perhaps he took it so for granted that he never considered that you didn't know, just as I took it for granted.'

'How can you explain away the infinite size of this world, and the age of Earth? And the evolution of life?' he said triumphantly. 'There, how do you explain evolution? The undeniable record of the fossils. Of carbon-14 dating and potassium-argon dating? I read about these new discoveries in a magazine on that bus, and their evidence is scientifically irrefutable!'

He fell silent as the waitress picked up their empty glasses. As soon as she left, he opened his mouth, and then he closed it again. The TV above the bar was showing the news and there on the screen was a drawing of two faces.

He said to Anana, 'Look there!'

She turned just in time to see the screen before the drawing faded away.

'They looked like us!' she said.

'Yeah. Police composites,' he said. 'The hounds have really got the scent now! Take it easy! If we get up now, people might look at us. But if we sit here and mind our own business, as I hope the other customers are doing . . .'

If it had been a colour set, the resemblance would have been much less close, since they had dyed their hair. But in black and white, their pictures were almost photographic.

However, no one even looked at them and it was possible that no one except the drunks at the bar had seen the TV set. And they were not about to turn around and face them.

'What did that thing say?' Anana whispered, referring to the TV.

'I don't know. There was too much noise for me to hear it. And I can't ask anybody at the bar.'

He was having afterthoughts about his plans. Perhaps he should give up his idea of tricking Red Orc out of hiding. Some things were worth chancing, but with the police actively looking for him, and his and Anana's features in every home in California, he did not want to attract any attention at all. Besides, the idea had been one of those wild hares that leaped through the brier patches of his mind. It was fantastic, too imaginative, but for that very reason might have succeeded. Not now, though. The moment he put his plan into action, he would bring down Orc's men and the police, and Red Orc would not come out himself because he would know where Kickaha was.

'Put on the dark glasses now,' he said. 'Enough time has gone by that nobody'd get suspicious and connect us with the pictures.'

'You don't have to explain everything,' she said sharply. 'I'm not as unintelligent as your Earthwomen.'

He was silent for a moment. Within a few minutes, so many events had dropped on his head like so many anvils. He wanted desperately to pursue the question of the origin and nature of this universe, but there was no time. Survival, finding Wolff and Chryseis, and killing the Beller, these were the important issues. Just now, survival was the most demanding.

'We'll pick up some more luggage,' he said. 'And the bell, too. I may be able to use it later, who knows?'

He paid the bill, and they walked out. Ten minutes later, they had the bell. The metal worker had done a good enough job. The bell wouldn't stand a close-up inspection by any Lord, of course. But at a reasonable distance, or viewed by someone unfamiliar with it, it would pass for the prized possession of a Beller. It was bell-shaped but the bottom was covered, was one and a half times the size of Kickaha's head, was made of aluminium, and had been sprayed with a quick-dry paint. Kickaha paid the maker of it and put the bell in the hatbox he had gotten from the shop.

A half hour later they walked across MacArthur Park.

Besides the soap-box speakers, there were a number of winos, hippie types, and some motorcycle toughs. And many people who seemed to be there just to enjoy the grass or to watch the unconventionals.

As they rounded a big bush, they stopped.

To their right was a concrete bench. On it sat two bristly-faced, sunken-cheeked, blue-veined winos and a young man. The young man was a well-built fellow with long dirty blond hair and a beard of about three days' growth. He wore clothes that were even dirtier and more ragged than the winos'.

A cardboard carton about a foot and a half square was on the bench by his side.

Anana started to say something and then she stopped.

Her skin turned pale, her eyes widened, she clutched her throat, and she screamed.

The alarm embedded in her brain, the alarm she had carried since she had become an adult ten thousand years ago, was the only thing that could be responsible for this terror.

Nearness to the bell of a Beller touched off that device in her brain. Her nerves wailed as if a siren had been tied into them. The ages-long dread of the Beller had seized her.

The blond man leaped up, grabbed the cardboard box, and ran away.

Kickaha ran after him. Anana screamed. The winos shouted, and many people came running.

At another time, he would have laughed. He had originally planned to take his box and the pseudo-bell into some such place as this, a park where winos and derelicts hung out, and create some kind of commotion, which would make the newspapers. That would have brought Red Orc out of his hole, Kickaha had hoped.

Ironically, he had stumbled across the real Beller.

If the Beller had been intelligent enough to cache his bell some place, he would have been safe. Kickaha and Anana would have passed him and never known.

Suddenly, he stopped running. Why chase the Beller, even if he could catch up with him? A chase would draw too much attention.

He took out the beamer disguised as a pen and set the little slide on its barrel for a very narrow flesh-piercing beam. He aimed it at the back of the Beller and, at that moment, as if the Beller realized what must happen, he dropped to the ground. His box went tumbling, he rolled away and then disappeared behind a slight ridge. Kickaha's beam passed over him, struck a tree, drilled a hole into it. Smoke poured out of the bark. Kickaha shut the beamer off. If it was kept on for more than a few seconds, it needed another powerpack.

The Beller's head popped up, and his hand came out with a slender dark object in it. He pointed it at Kickaha, who leaped into the air sideways and at the same time threw the hatbox away. There was a flash of something white along the box, and the box and its contents, both split in half, fell to the ground. The hatbox burst into flames just before it struck.

Kickaha threw himself onto the ground and shot once. The grass on the ridge became brown. The next instant, the Beller was shooting again. Kickaha rolled away and then was up and away, zigzagging.

Anana was running towards him, her hand held up with the huge ring pointed forward. Kickaha whirled to aid her and saw that the Beller, who had retrieved the cardboard box, was running away again. Across the grass towards them, from all sides, people were running. Among them were two policemen.

Kickaha thought that his antics and those of the Beller must have seemed very peculiar to the witnesses. Here were these two youths, each with a box, pointing ballpoint pens at each other, dodging, ducking, playing cowboy and Indian. And the woman who had been screaming as if she had suddenly seen Frankenstein's monster was now in the game.

One of the policemen shouted at them.

Kickaha said, 'Don't let them catch us! We'll be done for! Get the Beller!'

They began running at top speed. The cops shouted some more. He looked behind him. Neither had their guns out but it would not be long before they did.

They were overtaking the Beller, and the policemen were dropping behind. He was breathing too hard, though.

Whatever his condition, the Beller's was worse. He was slowing down fast. This meant that very shortly he would turn again, and Kickaha had better be nimble. In a few seconds, he would have the Beller within range of the beamer, and he would take both legs off. And that would be the end of possibly the greatest peril to man, other than man himself, of course.

The Beller ran up concrete steps in a spurt of frantic energy and onto the street above. Kickaha slowed down and stopped before ascending the last few steps. He expected the Beller to be waiting for his head to appear. Anana came up behind him then. Between deep gasps, she said, 'Where is he?'

'If I knew, I wouldn't be standing here,' he said.

He turned and left the steps to run crouching across the steep slope of the hill. When he was about forty feet away from the steps, he got down on his belly and crawled up to the top of the slope. The Beller would be wondering what he was doing. If he were intelligent, he would know that Kickaha wasn't going to charge up and over the steps. He'd be looking on both sides of the steps for his enemy to pop up.

Kickaha looked to his right. Anana had caught on and was also snaking along. She turned her head and grinned at him and waved. He signalled that they should both look over the edge at the same time. If the Beller was paralysed for just a second by the double appearance, and couldn't make up his mind which one to shoot at first, he was as good as dead.

That is, if the cops behind them didn't interfere. Their shouts were getting louder, and then a gun barked and the dirt near Kickaha flew up.

He signalled, and they both stuck their heads up. At that moment, a gun cracked in the street before them.

The Beller was down on his back in the middle of the street. There was a car beside him, a big black Lincoln, and several men were about to pick the Beller up and load him into the car. One of the men was Kleist.

Kickaha swore. He had run the Beller right into the arms of Orc's men, who were probably cruising this area and looking for a man with a big box. Or maybe somebody had – oh, irony of ironies – seen Kickaha with his box and thought he was the Beller!

He gestured at Anana and they both jumped up and ran off towards the car. More shouts but no shots from the policemen. The men by the limousine looked up just as they hurled the limp form of the Beller into the car. They climbed in, and the car shot away with a screaming of burning rubber into the temporarily opened lane before it.

Kickaha aimed at the back of the car, hoping to pierce a tyre or to set the gasoline tank on fire. Nothing happened, and the car was gone yowling around a corner. His beamer was empty.

There was nothing to do except to run once more, and now the policemen would be calling in for help. The only advantage for the runners was the very heavy rush hour traffic. The cops wouldn't be able to get here too fast in automobiles.

A half hour later, they were in a taxi, and, in another twenty minutes, they were outside a motel. The manager looked at them curiously and raised his eyebrows when he saw no luggage. Kickaha said that they were advance agents for a small rock group and their baggage was coming along later. They'd flown in on fifteen minutes' notice from San Francisco.

They took the keys to their room and went down the court and into their room. Here they lay down on the twin beds and, after locking the door and pushing the bureau against it, slept for fifteen minutes. On awakening, they took a shower and put their sweaty clothes back on. Following the manager's directions, they walked down to a shopping area and purchased some more clothes and necessary items.

'If we keep buying clothes and losing them the same day,' Kickaha said, 'we're going to go broke. And I'll have to turn to robbery again.'

When they returned to the motel room, he eagerly opened the latest copy of the *Los Angeles Times* to the personals column. He read down and then, suddenly, said, 'Yay!' and leaped into the air. Anana sat up from the bed and said, 'What's the matter?'

'Nothing's the matter! This is the first good thing that's happened since we got here! I didn't really believe that it'd work! But he's a crafty old fox, that Wolff! He thinks like me! Look, Anana!'

He shoved the paper at her. Blinking, she moved away so she could focus and then slowly read the words:

Hrowakas Kid. You came through. Stats. Wilshire and San Vicente. 9 p.m. C sends love.

Kickaha pulled her up off the bed and danced her around the room. 'We did it! We did it! Once we're all together, nothing'll stop us!'

Anana hugged and kissed him and said, 'I'm very happy. Maybe you're right, this is the turning point. My brother Jadawin! Once I would have tried to kill him. But no more. I can hardly wait.'

'Well, we won't have long to wait,' he said. He forced himself to become sober. 'I better find out what's going on.'

He turned the TV on. The newscaster of one station apparently was not going to mention them, so Kickaha switched channels. A minute later, he was rewarded.

He and Anana were wanted for questioning about the kidnapping of Kleist. The manager of the motel in which

Kleist had been tied up had described the two alleged kidnappers. Kleist himself had made no charges at first, but then Cambring's body had been found. The police had made a connection between Cambring and Kickaha and Anana because of the ruckus at the La Brea Tar Pits. There was also an additional charge: the stealing of Cambring's car.

Kickaha did not like the news but he could not help chuckling a little because of the frustration that Red Orc must feel. The Lord would have wanted some less serious charge, such as the car stealing only, so that he could pay the bail of the two and thus nab them when they walked out of the police station. But on charges such as kidnapping, he might not be able to get them released.

These charges were serious enough, though not enough to warrant their pictures and descriptions on TV newscasts. What made this case so interesting was that the fingerprints of the male in the case had checked out as those of Paul Janus Finnegan, an ex-serviceman who had disappeared in 1946 from his apartment in Bloomington, Indiana, where he had been attending the university.

Twenty-four years later, he had showed up in Van Nuys, California, in very mysterious, or questionable, circumstances. And this was the kicker according to the newscaster – Finnegan was described by witnesses as being about twenty-five, yet he was fifty-two years old!

Moreover, since the first showing of his picture over TV, he had been identified as one of the men in a very mysterious chase in MacArthur Park.

The newscaster ended with a comment supposed to be droll. Perhaps this Finnegan had returned from the Fountain of Youth. Or perhaps the witnesses may have been drinking from a slightly different fountain.

'With all this publicity,' Kickaha said, 'We're in a bad spot. I hope the motel manager didn't watch this show.'

It was eight thirty. They were to meet Wolff at nine at Stats Restaurant on Wilshire and San Vicente. If they took a taxi, they could get there with plenty of time to spare. He decided they should walk, he did not trust the taxis. And while he would use them if he had to, he saw no reason to take one just to avoid a walk. Especially since they needed the exercise.

Anana complained that she was hungry and would like to get to the restaurant as soon as possible. He told her that suffering was good for the soul and grinned as he said it. His own belly was contracting with pangs, and his ribs felt more obtrusive than several days ago. But he was not going to be rushed into anything if he could help it.

While they walked, Kickaha questioned her about Red Orc and the 'alleged' creation of Earth.

'There was the universe of the Lords in the beginning, and that was the only one we knew about. Then, after ten thousand years of civilization, my ancestors formulated the theory of artificial universes. Once the mathematics of the concept was realized, it was only a matter of time and will until the first pocket universe was made. Then the same "space" would hold two worlds of space-matter, but one would be impervious to the inhabitants of the other, because each universe was "at right angles to the other". You realize that the term "right angles" does not mean anything. It is just an attempt to explain something that can really only be explained to one who understands the mathematics of the concept. I myself though I designed a universe of my own and then built it, never understood the mathematics or even how the world-making machines operated.

'The first artificial universe was constructed about two hundred years before I was born. It was made by a group of Lords – they did not call themselves Lords then, by the way – among whom were my father Urizen and his brother Orc. Orc had already lived the equivalent of two thousand Terrestrial years. He had been a physicist and then a biologist and finally a social scientist.

'The initial step was like blowing a balloon in non-space. Can you conceive that? I can't either, but that's the way it was explained to me. You blow a balloon in non-space. That is, you create a small space or a small universe, one to which you can "gate" your machines. These expand the space next to, or in, the time-space of the original universe. The new world is expanded so that you can gate even larger machines into it. And these expand the universe more, and you gate more machines into the new larger space.

‘From the beginning of this making of a new world, you have set up a world which may have quite different physical “laws” than the original universe. It’s a matter of shaping the space-time-matter so that, say, gravity works differently than in the original world.

‘However, the first new universe was crude, you might say. It embodied no new principles. It was, in fact, an exact imitation of the original. Well, not exact in the sense that it was not a copy of the world as it was but as it had been in our past.’

‘The copy was this – my – world?’ Kickaha said ‘Earth’s?’

She nodded and said, ‘It – this universe – was the first. And it was made approximately fifteen thousand Earth years ago. This solar system deviated only in small particulars from the solar system of the Lords. This Earth deviated only slightly from the native planet of the Lords.’

‘You mean . . .?’

He was silent while they walked a half block, then he said, ‘So that explains what they meant when you said this world was fairly recent. I knew that that could not be so, because potassium-argon and xenon-argon dating prove irrefutably that this world is more than two and a half billion years old, and hominid fossils have been found which are at least one million seven hundred and fifty thousand years old. And then we have carbon-14 dating, which is supposed to be accurate up to fifty thousand years ago, if I remember that article correctly.

‘But you’re saying that the rocks of your world, which were four and a half billion years old, were reproduced in this universe. And so, though they were really made only fifteen thousand years ago, they would seem to be four and a half billion years old.

‘And we find fossils which prove indubitably that dinosaurs lived sixty million years ago, and we find stone tools and the skeletons of men who lived a million years ago. But these were duplicated from your world.'

'That is exactly right.' she said.

'But the stars!' he said. 'The galaxies, the super-novas, the quasars, the millions, billions of them, billions of light-years away! The millions of stars in this galaxy alone, which is one hundred thousand light-years across! The red shift of light from galaxies receding from us at a quarter of the speed of light and billions of light-years away! The radio stars, the – my God, everything!'

He threw his hands up to indicate the infinity and eternity of the universe. And also to indicate the utter nonsense of her words.

'This universe is the first, and the largest, of the artificial ones,' she said. 'Well, not the largest, the second one was just as large. Its diameter is three times that of the distance from the sun to the planet Pluto. If men ever build a ship to voyage to the nearest star, they will get past the orbit of Pluto and then to a distance twice that of Pluto from the sun. And then . . .'

'Then?'

'And then the ship will enter an area where it will be destroyed. It will run into a – what shall I call it? – a force field is the only term I can think of. And it would disappear in a blaze of energy. And so will any other ship, or ships, coming after it. The stars are not for men. Mainly because there are no stars.'

Kickaha wanted to protest violently. He felt outraged. But he forced himself to say calmly, 'How do you explain that?'

'The space-matter outside the orbit of Pluto is a simulacrum. A tiny simulacrum. Relatively tiny, that is.'

'The effects of the light from the stars, the nebulas, and so forth? The red shift? The speed of light? All that.'

'There's a warping factor which gives all the necessary illusions.'

All extra-Plutonian astronomy, all cosmogony, all cosmology, was false.

'But why did the Lords feel it necessary to set up this simulacrum of an infinite ever-expanding universe with its trillions of heavenly bodies? Why didn't they just leave the sky blank except for the moon and the planets? Why this utterly cruel deception. Or need I ask? I had forgotten for the moment that the Lords are *cruel.*'

She patted his hand, looked up into his eyes, and said, 'The Lords are not the only cruel ones. You forget that I told you that this universe was an exact copy of ours. I meant exact. From the centre, that is, the sun, to the outer walls of this universe, your world is a duplicate of ours. That includes the simulacrum of extra-solar-system space.'

He stopped and said, 'You mean...? The native world of the Lords was an artificial universe, too?'

'Yes. After three ships had been sent out past our outermost planet, to the nearest star, only four-point-three light-years away – we thought – a fourth ship was sent. But this slowed down when it came near the area where the others had disappeared in a burst of light. It was not destroyed, but it could progress no further than the first three. It was repelled by a force field. Or was turned away by the structure of the space-matter continuum at that point.

'After some study, we reluctantly came to the realization that there were no stars or outer space. Not as we had thought of them.

'This revelation was not accepted by many people. In fact, the impact of this discovery was so great that our civilization was in a near-psychotic state for a long while.

'Some historians have maintained that it was the discovery that we were in an artificial, comparatively finite, universe that spurred us – stung us – into searching for means of making our own synthetic universes. Because, if we were ourselves the product of a people who made our universe, and, therefore, made us, then we, too, could make our worlds. And so...'

'Then Earth's world is not even secondhand!' Kickaha said. 'It's thirdhand! But who could have made your world? Who are the Lords of the Lords?'

'So far, we do not know,' she said. 'We have found no

trace of them or their native worlds or any other artificial worlds they might have made. They exist on a plane of polarity that was beyond us then, and, as far as I know, will always be beyond us.'

Kickaha thought that this discovery should have humbled the Lords. Perhaps, in the beginning, it did. But they had recovered and gone on to their own making of cosmoses and their solipsist way of life.

And in their search for immortality, they had made the Bellers, those Frankenstein's monsters, and then, after a long war, had conquered the Bellers and disposed of the menace forever – they had thought. But now there was a Beller loose and ... No, he was not loose. He was in the hands of Red Orc, who surely would see to it that the Beller died and his bell was buried deep somewhere, perhaps at the bottom of the Pacific.

'I'll swallow what you told me,' he said, 'though I'm choking. But what about the people of Earth? Where did they come from?'

'Your ancestors of fifteen thousand years ago were made in the biolabs of the Lords. One set was made for this Earth and another set, exact duplicates, for the second Earth. Red Orc made two universes which were alike, and he put down on the face of each Earth the same peoples. Exactly the same in every detail.

'Orc set down in various places the infants, the Caucasoids, the Negroids and Negritos, the Mongolians, Amerinds, and Australoids. These were infants who were raised by Lords to be Stone Age peoples. Each group was taught a language, which, by the way, were artificial languages. They were also taught how to make stone and wooden tools, how to hunt, what rules of behaviour to adopt, and so forth. And then the Lords disappeared. Most of them returned to the home universe, where they would make plans for building their own universes. Some stayed on the two Earths to see but not be seen. Eventually, all of these were killed or run out of the two universes by Red Orc, but that was a thousand years later.'

'Wait a minute,' Kickaha said. 'I never thought about it,

just took it for granted, I guess. But I thought all Lords were Caucasians.'

'That is just because it so happened that you only met Caucasoid Lords,' she said. 'How many have you met, by the way?'

He grinned and said, 'Six.'

'I would guess that there are about a thousand left, and of these about a third are Negroid and a third Mongolian, to use Terrestrial terms. On our world our equivalent of Australoids became extinct and our equivalent of Polynesians and Amerinds became absorbed by the Mongolians and Caucasoids.'

'That other Earth universe?' he said. 'Have the peoples there developed on lines similar to ours? Or have they deviated considerably'

'I couldn't tell you,' she said. 'Only Red Orc knows.'

He had many questions, including why there happened to be a number of gates on Earth over which Red Orc had no control. It occurred to him that these might be gates left over from the old days when many Lords were on Earth.

There was no time to ask more questions. They were crossing San Vicente at Wilshire now, and Stats was only a few dozen yards away. It was a low brick and stone building with a big plate glass window in front. His heart was beating fast. The prospect of seeing Wolff and Chryseis again made him happier than he had been for a long time. Nevertheless, he did not lose his wariness.

'We'll walk right on by the first time,' he said. 'Let's case it.'

They were opposite the restaurant. There were about a dozen people eating in it, two waitresses, and a woman at the cash register. Two uniformed policemen were in a booth; their black and white car was in the plaza parking lot west of the building. Neither Wolff nor Chryseis was there.

It was still not quite nine o'clock, however, and Wolff might be approaching cautiously.

They halted before the display window of a dress shop.

From their vantage point, they could observe anybody entering or leaving the restaurant. Two customers got up and walked out. The policemen showed no signs of leaving. A car drove into the plaza, pulled into a slot, and turned its lights out. A man and a woman, both white-haired, got out and went in to the restaurant. The man was too short and skinny to be Wolff, and the woman was too tall and bulky to be Chryseis.

A half hour passed. More customers arrived and more left. None of them could be his friends. At a quarter to ten, the two policemen left.

Anana said, 'Could we go inside now? I'm so hungry, my stomach is eating itself.'

'I don't like the smell of this,' he said. 'Nothing looks wrong, except Wolff not being here yet. We'll wait a while, give him a chance to show. But we're not going inside that place. It's too much like a trap.'

'I see a restaurant way down the street,' she said. 'Why don't I go down there and get some food and bring it back?'

They went over her pronunciation of two cheeseburgers, everything except onions, and two chocolate milk shakes, very thick. To go. He told her what to expect in change and then told her to hurry.

For a minute, he wondered if he should not tell her to forget it. If something unexpected happened, and he had to take off without her, she'd be in trouble. She still did not know the way of this world.

On the other hand, his own belly was growling.

Reluctantly he said, 'Okay. But don't be long, and if anything happens so we get separated, we'll meet back at the motel.'

He alternated watching the restaurant to his left and looking down the street for her.

About five minutes later she appeared with a large white paper bag. She crossed the street twice to get back on the same block and started walking toward him. She had taken a few steps from the corner when a car which had passed her stopped. Two men jumped out and ran towards her. Kickaha began running towards them. Anana dropped the bag and then she crumpled. There was no sound of a gun or spurt of flame or anything to indicate that a gun had been used. The two men ran to her. One picked her up; the other turned to face Kickaha.

At the same time, another man got out of the car and ran towards Kickaha. Several cars came up behind the stopped car, honked, and then pulled around it. Their lights revealed one man inside the parked car in the driver's seat.

Kickaha leaped sideways and out into the street. A car blew its horn and swerved away to keep from hitting him. The angry voice of its driver floated back, 'You crazy son . . .!'

Kickaha had his beamer-pen out by then. A few hasty words set it for piercing effect. His first concern was to keep from being hit by the beamers of the men and his second was to cripple the car.

He dropped on the street and rolled, catching out of the corner of his eye a flash of needle-thin, sun-hot ray. A beam leaped from his own pen and ran along the wheels of the car on the street side. The tyres blew with a bang, and the car listed to one side as the bottom parts of the wheels fell off.

The driver jumped out and ran behind the car.

Kickaha was up and running across the street towards a car parked by the kerb. He threw himself forward, hit the macadam hard, and rolled. When he had crawled behind the car and peered from behind it, he saw that a second car was stopped some distance behind the first. Anana was being passed into it by the men from the first car.

He jumped up and shouted, but several cars whizzed by, preventing him from using the beam. By the time they had passed, the second car was making a U-turn. More cars, coming down the other lane, passed between him and the automobile containing her. He had no chance now to beam the back wheels of the departing car. And just then, as if the Fates were against him, a police car approached on the lane on his side and stopped. Kickaha knew that he could not be questioned. Raging, he fled.

Behind him, a siren started whooping. A man shouted at him, and fired into the air.

He increased his pace, and ran out onto San Vicente, almost stopping traffic as he dodged between the streaming cars. He crossed the divider, and as he reached the other side of the street; he spared a glance behind and saw one policeman on the divider, blocked by the stream of cars.

The police car had made a U-turn and was coming across. Kickaha ran on, turned the corner, ran between two houses, and came out behind them on San Vicente again. The cop on foot was getting into the car. Kickaha crouched in the shadows until the car, siren still whooping, took off again. It went around the same corner he had turned.

He doubled to Stats and looked inside. There was no sign of Wolff or Chryseis. Another police car was approaching, its lights flashing but its siren quiet.

He went across the parking lot and around a building. It took him an hour, but by then, dodging between houses, running across streets, hiding now and then, he had eluded the patrol cars. After a stop at a drive-in to pick up some food, he returned to his motel.

There was a police car parked outside it. Once more, he abandoned his luggage and was gone into the night.

There was one thing he had to do immediately. He knew that Red Orc would give Anana a drug which would make her answer any question Orc asked. It just might happen that Orc would become aware that the Horn of Shambarimen had been brought through into this world and that it now was in a locker in the downtown bus station. He would, of course, send men down to the station, and would not hesitate to have the whole station blown up. Orc would not care what he had to do to get that Horn.

Kickaha caught a taxi and went down to the bus station. After emptying the locker, he walked seven blocks from the bus station before he took another taxi, which carried him to the downtown railroad station. Here he placed the Horn in a locker. He did not want to carry the key with him. He purchased a package of gum and chewed all the sticks until he had a big ball of gum. While he was chewing, he strolled around outside the station, inspected a tree on the edge of the parking lot, and decided he had found an excellent hiding place. He stuck the key, embedded in the ball of gum, into a small hollow in the tree just above the line of his vision.

He took another taxi to the Sunset and Fairfax area.

He awoke about eight o'clock on an old mattress on the bare floor of a big mouldy room. Beside him slept Rod (short for Rodriga). Rodriga Elseed, as she called herself, was a tall thin girl with remarkably large breasts, a pretty but overfreckled face, big dark-blue eyes, and lank yellow-brown hair that fell to her waist. She was wearing a red-and-blue checked lumberman's shirt, dirty bell-bottoms, and torn moccasins. Her teeth were white and even, but her breath reeked of too little food and too much marijuana.

While walking along Sunset Boulevard in the Saturday night crowds, Kickaha had seen her sitting on the sidewalk talking to another girl and a boy.

The girl, seeing Kickaha, had smiled at him. She said, 'Hello, friend. You look as if you've been running for a long time.'

'I hope not,' he said, smiling back. 'The fuzz might see it, too.'

It had been easy to make the acquaintanceship of all three, and when Kickaha said he would buy them something to eat he felt a definite strengthening of their interest.

After eating they had wandered around Sunset, 'grooving' on everything. He learned much about their sub-world that night. When he mentioned that he had no roof over his head, they invited him to stay at their pad. It was a big run-down spooky old house, they said, with about fifty people, give or take ten, living in it and chipping in on the rent and utilities, if they had it. If they didn't they were welcome until they got some bread.

Rodriga Elseed (he was sure that wasn't her real name) had recently come here from Dayton, Ohio. She had left two uptight parents there. She was seventeen and didn't know what she wanted to be. Just herself for the time being, she said.

Kickaha donated some more money for marijuana, and the other girl, Jackie, disappeared for a while. When she returned, they went to the big house, which they called the Shire, and retired to this room. Kickaha smoked with them, since he had the feeling that he would be a far more accepted comrade if he did. The smoke did not seem to do much except to set him coughing.

After a while, Jackie and the boy, Dar, began to make love. Rodriga and Kickaha went for a walk. She said she liked Kickaha, but did not feel like going to bed with him on such short acquaintance.

Kickaha said that he understood. He was not at all disgruntled. He just wanted to get some sleep. An hour later, they returned to the room, which was then empty and fell asleep on the dirty mattress.

But the night's sleep had not lessened his anxiety. He was depressed because Anana was in Red Orc's hands, and he suspected that Wolff and Chryseis were also his prisoners. Somehow, Red Orc had guessed that the ad was from Kickaha and had answered. But he would not have been able to answer so specifically unless he had Wolff and had gotten out of him what he knew about Kickaha.

Knowing the Lords, Kickaha felt it was likely that Red Orc would torture Wolff and Chryseis first, even though he had only to administer a drug which would make them tell whatever Orc asked for. After that, he would torture them again and finally kill them.

He would do the same with Anana. Even now . . .

He shuddered and said, 'No!'

Rodriga opened her eyes and said, 'What?'

'Go back to sleep,' he said, but she sat up and hugged her knees to her breasts. She rocked back and forth and said, 'Something is bugging you, *amigo*. Deeply. Look, I don't want to bug you, too, but if there's anything I can do . . .'

'I've got my own thing to do,' he said.

He could not involve her in this even if she could help

him in any way. She would be killed the first time they contacted Red Orc's men. She wasn't the fast, extremely tough, many-resourced woman that Anana was. Yes, that's right, he said to himself. *Was.* She might not be alive at this very moment.

Tears came to his eyes.

'Thanks, Rod. I've got to be going now. Dig you later, maybe.'

She was up off the floor then and said, 'There's something a little strange about you, Paul. You're young but you don't use our lingo quite right, you know what I mean? You seem to me to be just a little weird. I don't mean a creep. I mean, as if you don't quite belong to this world, I know how that is; I get the same feeling quite a lot. That is, I don't belong here, either. But it isn't quite the same thing with you, I mean, you are *really* out of this world. You aren't some being off a flying saucer, are you now?'

'Look, Rod, I appreciate your offer. I really do. But you can't go with me or do anything for me. Not just now. But later, if anything comes up that you can help me with, I sure as hell will let you do something for me and be glad to do so.'

He bent over and kissed her forehead and said, '*Hasta la vista*, Rodriga. Maybe *adiós*. Let's hope we see each other again, though.'

Kickaha walked until he found a small restaurant. As he ate breakfast he considered the situation.

One thing was certain. The problem of the Beller was solved. It did not matter whether Kickaha or Orc killed him. Just so he was killed and the Bellers forever out of the way.

And Red Orc now had all but one of his enemies in his hands, and he would soon have that last one. Unless that enemy got to him first. Red Orc had not been using all his powers to catch Kickaha because his first concern was the Beller. But now, he could concentrate on the last holdout.

Somehow, Kickaha had to find the Lord before the Lord got to him. Very soon.

When he had finished eating, he bought a *Times*. As he

walked along the street, he scanned the columns of the paper. There was nothing about a girl being kidnapped or a car on Wilshire with the bottom halves of the left wheels sliced off. There was a small item about the police sighting Paul J. Finnegan, the mystery man, his getting away, and a résumé of what was known about him in his pre-1946 life.

He forced himself to settle down and to think calmly. Never before had he been so agitated. He was powerless to stop the very probable torture of his lover and his friends, which might be happening right now.

There *was* no way to get into the Lord's house and face him. If he gave himself up, he could then rely upon his inventiveness and his boldness after he was brought before the Lord.

His sense of reality rescued him. He would be taken in only after a thorough examination to make sure he had no hidden weapons or devices. And he would be brought in bound and helpless.

Unless the Lord followed the custom of always leaving some way open for an exceptionally intelligent and skilled man. Always, no matter how effective and powerful the traps the Lords set about their palaces, they left at least one route open, if the invader was perceptive and audacious enough. That was the rule of the deadly game they had played for thousands of years. It was, in fact, this very rule that had made Red Orc leave the gate in the cave unguarded and untrapped.

Because he had nothing else to do, he went into a public phone booth on a gas station lot and dialled Cambring's number. The phone was picked up so swiftly that Kickaha felt, for a second, that Cambring was still alive and was waiting for his call. It was Cambring's wife who answered, however.

Kickaha said, 'Paul Finnegan speaking.'

There was a pause and then, 'You murderer!' she screamed.

He waited until she was through yelling and cursing him and was sobbing and gasping.

'I didn't kill your husband,' he said, 'although I would have been justified if I had, as you well know. It was the big boss who killed him.'

'You're a liar!' she screamed.

'Tell your big boss I want to speak to him. I'll wait on this line. I know you have several phones you can use.'

'Why should I do that?' she said. 'I'll do nothing for you!'

'I'll put it this way. If he gets his hands on me, he'll see to it that you get your revenge. But if I don't get into contact with him, right now, I'm taking off for the great unknown. And he'll never find me.'

She said, 'All right,' sniffled, and was gone. About sixty seconds later, she was back. 'I got a loudspeaker here, a box, what you call it?' she said. 'Anyway, you can speak to him through it.'

Kickaha doubted that the man he was going to talk to was actually the 'big boss' himself. Although, Mrs. Cambring had revealed that she now had information that she had not possessed when he had drugged her. Could this be because the Lord had calculated that Kickaha would call her?

He felt a chill sweep over the back of his scalp. If Red Orc could anticipate him this well, then he would also know Kickaha's next step.

He shrugged. There was only one way to find out if Red Orc was that clever.

The voice was deep and resonant. Its pronunciation of English was that of a native, and its use of vocabulary seemed to be 'right'. The speaker did not introduce himself. His tone indicated that he did not need to do so, that just hearing him should convince anyone immediately of his identity. And of his power.

Kickaha felt that this was truly Red Orc, and the longer he heard him, the more he identified certain characteristics that reminded him of Anana's voice. There was a resemblance there, which was not surprising, since the family of Urizen was very inbred.

'Finnegan! I have your friends Wolff and Chryseis and

your lover, my niece, Anana. They are well. Nothing has happened to them, nothing harmful, that is. As yet! I drugged the truth from them; they have told me everything they know about this.'

Then it is good, Kickaha thought, *that Anana does not know where the Horn of Shambarimen really is.*

There was a pause. Kickaha said, 'I'm listening.'

'I should kill them, after some suitable attentions, of course. But they don't really represent any threat to me; they were as easily caught as just-born rabbits.'

A Lord always had to do some bragging. Kickaha said nothing, knowing that the Lord would get to the point when he became short-winded. But Red Orc surprised him.

'I could wait until I caught you, and I would not have to wait very long. But just now time is of the essence, and so I am willing to make a trade.'

He paused again. Kickaha said, 'I'm all ears.'

'I will let the prisoners go and will allow them to return to Jadawin's world. And you may go with them. But on several conditions. First, you will hand over the Horn of Shambarimen to me!'

Kickaha had expected this. The Horn was not only unique in all the universes, it was the most prized item of the Lords. It had been made by the fabled ancestor of all the Lords now living, though it had been in the possession of his equally fabled son so long that it was sometimes referred to as the Horn of Ilmarwolkin. It had a unique utility among gates. It could be used alone. All other gates had to exist in pairs. There had to be one in the universe to be left and a sister, a resonant gate, in the universe to be entered. The majority of these were fixed, though the crescent type was mobile. But the Horn had only to be blown upon, with the keys of the Horn played in the proper coded sequence, and a momentary way between the universes would open. That is, it would do so if the Horn were played near a 'resonant' point in the 'walls' between the two worlds.

A resonant point was the path between two universes, but these universes never varied. Thus, if a Lord used the

Horn without knowing where the resonant point would lead him, he would find himself in whichever universe was on the other side, like it or not.

Kickaha knew of four places where he could blow the Horn and be guaranteed to open the way to the World of Tiers. One was at the gate in the cave near Lake Arrowhead. One was in Kentucky, but he would need Wolff to guide him to it. Another would be in his former apartment in Bloomington, Indiana. And the fourth would be in the closet in the basement of a house in Tempe, Arizona. Wolff knew that, too, but he had described to Kickaha how to get to it from Earth's side, and Kickaha had not forgotten.

Red Orc's voice was impatient. 'Come, come! Don't play games with *me*, Earthling! Say yes or say no, but be quick about it!'

'Yes! Provisionally, that is. It depends upon your other conditions.'

'I have only one.' Red Orc coughed several times and then said, 'And that is, that you and the others first help me catch the Beller!'

Kickaha was shocked, but a thousand experiences in being surprised enabled him to conceal it. Smoothly, he said 'Agreed! In fact, that's something I had wished you would agree to do, but at that time I didn't see working with you. Of course, you had no whip hand then.'

So the Beller had either been caught by Orc's men and had then escaped or somebody else had captured him. That somebody else could only be another Lord.

Or perhaps it was another Beller.

At that thought, he became cold.

'What do we do now?' he said, unwilling to state the truth, which was, 'What do *you* wish now?'

Orc's voice became crisp and restrainedly triumphant.

'You will present yourself at Mrs. Cambring's house as soon as possible, and my men will conduct you here. How long will it take you to get to Cambring's?'

'About half an hour,' Kickaha said. If he could get a

taxi at once, he could be there in ten minutes, but he wanted a little more time to plan.

'Very well!' the Lord said. 'You must surrender all arms, and you will be thoroughly examined by my men. Understood?'

'Oh, sure.'

While he was talking, he had been as vigilant as a bird. He looked out the glass of the booth for anything suspicious, but had seen nothing except cars passing. Now a car stopped by the kerb. It was a big dark Cadillac with a single occupant. The man sat for a minute, looked at his wristwatch, and then opened the door and got out. He sauntered towards the booth, looking again at his watch. He was a very well-built youth about six-foot-three and dressed modishly and expensively. The long yellow hair glinted in the sun as if it were flecked with gold. His face was handsome but rugged.

He stopped near the booth and pulled a cigarette case from his jacket. Kickaha continued to listen to the instructions from the phone but he kept his eye on the newcomer. The fellow looked at the world through half-lidded arrogant eyes. He was evidently impatient because the booth was occupied. He glanced at his watch again and then lit his cigarette with a pass of the flame over the tip and a flicking away of the match in one smooth movement.

Kickaha spoke the code which prepared the ring on his finger to be activated for a short piercing beam. He would have to cut through the glass if the fellow were after him.

The voice on the phone kept on and on. It seemed as if he were dictating the terms of surrender to a great nation instead of to a single man. Kickaha must approach the front of the Cambring house and advance only halfway up the front walk and then stand until three men came out of the house and three men in a car parked across the street approached him from behind at the same time. And then . . .

The man outside the booth made a disgusted face as he looked at his watch again and swung away. Evidently he had given up on Kickaha.

But he only took two steps and spun, holding a snub-nosed handgun.

Kickaha dropped the phone and ducked, at the same time speaking the word which activated the ring.

The gun barked, the glass of the booth shattered, and Kickaha was enveloped in a white mist. It was so unexpected that he gasped once, knew immediately that he should hold his breath, and did so. He also lunged out of the booth, cutting down the door with the ring. The door fell outward from his weight, but he never heard it strike the ground.

When he recovered consciousness, he was in the dark and hard confines of a moving object. The odour of gas and the cramped space made him believe that he was in the trunk of a car. His hands were tied behind him, his legs were tied at the ankles, and his mouth was taped.

He was sweating from the heat, but there was enough air in the trunk. The car went up an incline and stopped. The motor stopped, doors squeaked, the car lifted as bodies left it, and then the lid of the trunk swung open. Four men were looking down at him, one of whom was the big youth who had fired the gas gun.

They pulled him out and carried him from the garage, the door of which was shut. The exit led directly into the hall of a house, which led to a large room, luxuriously furnished and carpeted. Another hall led them to a room with a ceiling a storey and a half high, an immense crystal chandelier, black and white parquet floor, heavy mahogany furniture, and paintings that looked like original old masters.

Here he was set down in a big high-backed chair and his legs were untied. Then he was told by one of the men to walk. A man behind urged him on with something hard and sharp against his back. He followed the others from the room through a doorway set under the great staircase. This led down a flight of twelve steps into a sparcely furnished room. At one end was a big massive iron door which he knew led to his prison cell. And so it was, though a rather comfortable prison. His hands were untied and the tape was taken from his mouth.

The beamer-ring had been removed, and the beamer-pen taken from his shirt pocket. While the big man watched, the others stripped him naked, cutting the shirt and his undershirt off. Then they explored his body cavities for weapons but found nothing.

He offered no resistance since it would have been futile.

The big man and another held guns on him. After the inspection, a man closed a shackle around one ankle. The shackle was attached to a chain which was fastened at the other end to a ring in the wall. The chain was very thin and lightweight and long enough to permit him to move anywhere in the room.

The big man smiled when he saw Kickaha eyeing it speculatively and said, 'It's a gossamer as a cobweb, my friend, but strong as the chain that bound Fenris.'

'I am Loki, not Fenris,' Kickaha said, grinning savagely. He knew that the man expected him to be ignorant of the reference to the great wolf of the old Norse religion, and he should have feigned ignorance. The less respect your imprisoner has for you, the more chance you have to escape. But he could not resist the answer.

The big man raised his eyebrows and said, 'Ah, yes. And you remember what happened to Loki?'

'I am also Logi' Kickaha said, but he decided that that sort of talk had gone far enough. He fell silent, waiting for the other to tell him who he was and what he meant to do.

The man did not look quite so young now. He seemed to be somewhat over thirty. His voice was heavy, smooth, and very authoritative. His eyes were beautiful; they were large and leaf-green and heavily lashed. His face seemed familiar, though Kickaha was sure that he had never seen it before.

The man gestured, and the others left the room. He closed the door behind him and then sat on the edge of the table. This was bolted down to the floor, as were the other pieces of furniture. He dangled one leg while he held his gun on his lap. It looked like a conventional weapon, not a gas gun or a disguised beamer, but Kickaha had no way of determining its exact type at that moment. He sat down on a chair and waited. It was true that this left the man looking down on him, but Kickaha was not one to allow a matter of relative altitude to give another a psychological advantage.

The man looked steadily at him for several minutes. Kickaha looked back and whistled softly.

'I've been following you for some time,' the man suddenly said. 'I still don't know who you are. Let me introduce myself. I am Red Orc.'

Kickaha stiffened, and he blinked.

The man smiled and said, 'Who did you think I was?'

'A Lord who'd gotten stuck in this universe and was looking for a way out,' Kickaha said. 'Are there two Red Orcs, then?'

The man lost some of his smile. 'No, there is only one! I am Red Orc! That other is an impostor! A usurper! I was careless for just one moment. But I got away with my life, and because of his bad luck, I will kill him and get back everything!'

'Who is that other?' Kickaha said. 'I had thought... but then he never named himself ... he let me think...'

That he was Red Orc, I thought so! But his name is Urthona, and he was once Lord of the Shifting World. Then that demon-bitch Vala, my niece, drove him from his world, and he fled and came here, to this world, my world. I did not know who it was, although I knew that some Lord had come through a gate in Europe. I hunted for him and did not find him and then I forgot about him. That was a thousand years ago; I presumed he had gotten out through some gate I did not know about or else had been killed.

'But he was lying low and all the time searching for me. And finally, only ten years ago, he found me, surveyed my fortress, my defences, watched my comings and my goings, and then he struck!

'I had grown careless, but I got away, although all my bodyguards died. And he took over. It was so simple for him because he was in the seat of power, and there was no one to deny him. How could there be anyone to say no to him? I had hidden my face too well. Anyone in the seat of power could issue orders, pull the strings, and he would be obeyed, since the Earthlings who are closest to him do not know his real name or his real face.

'And I could not go to the men who had carried out my orders and say, "Here I am, your own true Lord! Obey me and kill that fool who is now giving you orders!' I would have been shot down at once, because Urthona had described me to his servants, and they thought I was the enemy of their leader.

'So I went into hiding, just as Urthona had done. But when I strike, I will not miss! And I shall again be in the seat of power!'

There was a pause. Orc seemed to be expecting him to comment. Perhaps he expected praise or awe or terror.

Kickaha said, 'Now that he has this seat of power, as you call it, is he Lord of both Earths? Or of this one only?'

Orc seemed set aback by this question. He stared and then his face got red.

'What is that to you?' he finally said.

'I just thought that you might be satisfied with being Lord of the other Earth. Why not let this Urthona rule this world? It looks to me, from the short time I've been here, that this world is doomed. The humans are polluting the air and the water and, at any time, they may kill off all life on Earth with an atomic war. Apparently, you are not doing anything to prevent this. So why not let Urthona have this dying world while you keep the other?'

He paused and then said, 'Or is Earth Number Two in as bad a condition as this one?'

Red Orc's face had lost its redness. He smiled and said, 'No, the other is not as bad off. It's much more desirable, even though it got exactly the same start as this one. But your suggestion that I surrender this world shows you don't know much about us, *leblabbiy.*'

'I know enough,' Kickaha said. 'But even Lords change for the better, and I had hoped . . .'

'I will do nothing to interfere here except to protect myself,' Orc said. 'If this planet chokes to death on its man-made foulness, or if it all goes out in a thousand bursts of radiation, it will do so without any aid or hindrance from me. I am a scientist, and I do not influence the direction of natural development one way or another on the two planets. Anything I do is on a microscale level and will not disturb macroscale matters.

'That, by the way, is one more reason why I must kill anyone who invades my universes. They might decide to interfere with my grand experiments.'

'Not me!' Kickaha said. 'Not Wolff or Chryseis or Anana! All we want is to go back to our own worlds! After the Beller is killed, of course. He's the only reason we came here. You must believe that!'

'You don't really expect me to believe that?' Orc said.

Kickaha shrugged and said, 'It's true, but I don't expect you to believe it. You Lords are too paranoid to see things clearly.'

Red Orc stood up from the table. 'You will be kept prisoner here until I have captured the others and defeated Urthona. Then I'll decide what to do with you.'

By this, Kickaha knew, he meant just what delicate tortures he could inflict upon him. For a moment, he thought about informing Orc of the Horn of Shambarimen's presence on Earth in this area. Perhaps he could use it for a bargaining point. Then he decided against it. Once Orc knew that it was here, he would just get the information from his captive by torture or drugs.

'Have you killed the Beller yet?' he said.

Orc smiled and said, 'No.'

He seemed very pleased with himself. 'If it becomes necessary, I will threaten Urthona with him. I will tell Urthona that if he does not leave, I will let the Beller loose. That, you understand, is the most horrible thing a Lord could do.'

'You would do this? After what you said about getting rid of anybody that might interfere with the natural development?'

'If I knew that my own death was imminent, unavoidable, yes, I would! Why not? What do I care what happens to this world, to all the worlds, if I am dead? Serve them right!'

There were more questions to which Kickaha wanted answers, but he was not controlling the interview. Orc abruptly walked out, leaving by the other door. Kickaha strained at the end of the chain to see through it, but the door swung out towards him and so shut off his view.

He was left with only his thoughts, which were pessimistic. He had always boasted that he could get loose from any prison, but it was, after all, a boast. He had, so far, managed to escape from every place in which he had been imprisoned, but he knew that he would someday find himself in a room with no exit. This was probably it. He was being observed by monitors, electronic or human or both, the chain was unbreakable with bare hands, and it also could be the conductor for some disabling and punishing agent if he did not behave.

This did not prevent him from trying to break it and twist it apart, because he could not afford to take anything for granted. The chain was unharmed, and he supposed that any human monitors would be amused by his efforts.

He stopped struggling, and he used the toilet facilities. Then he lay down on the sofa and thought for a while about his predicament. Though he was naked, he was not uncomfortable. The air was just a few degrees below his body temperature and it moved slowly enough so that it did not chill him. He fell asleep after a while, having found no way out, having thought of no plan that could reasonably work.

When he awoke, the room was as before. The sourceless light still made it high noon, and the air had not changed temperature. However, on sitting up, he saw a tray with dishes and cups and table utensils on top of the small thin-legged wooden table at the end of the sofa. He did not think that anyone could have entered with it unless he had been drugged. It seemed more likely that a gate was embedded in the wooden top and that a tray had been gated through while he slept.

He ate hungrily. The utensils were made of wood, and

the dishes and the cups were of pewter and bore stylized octopuses, dolphins, and lobsters. After he ate, he walked back and forth within the range of the chain for about an hour. He tried to think of what he could do with the gate, if there was a gate inside that wooden table top. At the end of the hour, as he turned back towards the table, he saw that the tray was gone. His suspicion was correct; the top did contain a gate.

There had been no sound. The Lords of the old days had solved the problem of noise caused by sudden disappearance of an object. The air did not rush into the vacuum created by the disappearance because the gate arrangement included a simultaneous exchange of air between the gate on one end and that at the other.

About an hour later, Orc entered through the door by which he had left. He was accompanied by two men, one carrying a crossbow and the other carried a hypodermic needle. They wore kilts. One kilt was striped red and black and the other was white with a stylized black octopus with large blue eyes. Other than the kilts, leather sandals, and beads and metal medallions at the end of the necklace of beads, they wore nothing. Their skins were dark, their faces looked somewhat Mediterranean but also reminded him of Amerindians, and their straight black hair was twisted into two pigtails. One pigtail fell down the back and the other was coiled on the right side of the head.

Orc spoke to them in a language unknown to Kickaha. It did seem vaguely Hebrew or Arabic to him but that was only because of its sounds. He knew too little of either language to be able to identify them.

While the one with the crossbow stood to one side and aimed it at Kickaha, the other approached from the other side. Orc commanded him to submit to the injection, saying that if he resisted, the crossbow would shoot its hypodermic into him. And the pain that followed would be long-lasting and intense. Kickaha obeyed, since there was nothing else he could do.

He felt nothing following the injection. But he answered all of Orc's questions without hesitation. His brain did not feel clouded or bludgeoned. He was thinking as clearly as usual. It was just that he could not resist giving Orc all the information he asked for. But that was what kept him from mentioning the Horn of Shambarimen. Orc did not *ask* him about it nor was there any reason for him to do so. He had no knowledge that it had been in the possession of Wolff, or Jadawin, as Orc knew him.

Orc's questions did, however, reveal almost everything else of value to him. He knew something of Kickaha's life on Earth before that night in Bloomington when Paul Janus Finnegan had been accidentally catapulted out of this universe into the World of Tiers. He learned more about Finnegan's life since then, when Finnegan had become Kickaha (and also Horst von Horstmann and a dozen other identities). He learned about Wolff-Jadawin and Chryseis and Anana, the invasion of the Black Bellers, and other matters pertinent. He learned much about Kickaha's and Anana's activities since they had gated into the cavern near Lake Arrowhead.

Orc said, 'If I did allow you and Anana and Wolff and Chryseis to go back to your world, would you stay there and not try to get back here?'

'Yes,' Kickaha said. 'Provided that I knew for sure that the Beller was dead.'

'Hmm. But your World of Tiers sounds fascinating. Jadawin always was very creative. I think that I would like to add it to my possessions.'

This was what Kickaha expected.

Orc smiled again and said, 'I wonder what you would have done if you had found out where I used to live and where Urthona now sits in the seat of power.'

'I would have gone into it and killed you or Urthona,' Kickaha said. 'And I would have rescued Anana and Wolff and Chryseis and then searched for the Beller until I found him and killed him. And then we would have returned to my world, that is to Wolff's, to be exact.'

Orc looked thoughtful and paced back and forth for a while. Suddenly, he stopped and looked at Kickaha. He was smiling as if a brilliant idea were shining through him.

'You make yourself sound very tricky and resourceful,' he said. 'So tricky that I could almost think you were a Lord, not just a *leblabbiy* Earthling.'

'Anana has the crazy idea that I could be the son of a Lord,' Kickaha said. 'In fact, she thinks I could be your son.'

Orc said, 'What?' and he looked closely at Kickaha and then began laughing. When he had recovered, he wiped his eyes and said, 'That felt good! I haven't laughed like that for . . . how long? Never mind. So you really think *you* could be my child?'

'Not me, 'Kickaha said. 'Anana. And she likes to speculate about it because she still needs some justification for falling in love with a *leblabbiy*. If I could be half-Lord, then I'd be more acceptable. But this idea is one hundred percent wishful thinking, of course.'

'I have no children because I want to interfere as little as possible with the natural development here, although a child or two could really make little difference,' Orc said. 'But you could be the child of another Lord, I suppose. However, you've gotten me off the subject. I was saying that you were very tricky, if I am to believe your account of yourself. Perhaps I could use you.'

He fell silent again and paced back and forth once more with his head bent and his hands clasped behind him. Then he stopped, looked at Kickaha, and smiled. 'Why not? Let's see how good you are. I can't lose by it no matter what happens, and I may gain.'

Kickaha had guessed, correctly, what he was going to propose. He would tell him the address of Urthona, would take him there, in fact, provide him with some weapons, and allow him to attack Urthona as he wished. And if Kickaha failed, he still might so distract Urthona that Orc could take advantage of the distraction.

In any event, it would be amusing to watch a *leblabbiy* trying to invade the seat of power of a Lord.

'And if I do succeed?' Kickaha said.

'It's not very likely, since *I* have not had any success

yet. Though, of course, I haven't really tried yet. But if you should succeed, and I'm not worried that you will, I will permit you and your lover and your friends to return to your world. Provided that the others also swear, while under the influence of the proper drugs, that they have no intention of returning to either Earth.'

Kickaha did not believe this, but he saw no profit in telling Orc so. Once he was out of this cell and had some freedom of action – though closely watched by Orc – he would have some chance against the Lords.

Orc spoke the unknown language into a wristband device, and a moment later another entered. His kilt was red with a black stylized bird with a silver fish in its claws. He carried some papers which he gave to Orc, bowed, and withdrew.

Orc sat down by Kickaha.

The papers turned out to be maps of the central Los Angeles area and of Beverly Hills. Orc circled an area in Beverly Hills.

'That is the house where I lived and where Urthona now lives,' he said. 'The house you were searching for and where Anana and the others are now undoubtedly held. Or, at least, where they were taken after being captured.'

Orc's description of the defences in the house made Kickaha feel very vulnerable. It was true that Urthona would have changed the defence set-up in the house. But, though the configuration of the traps might be different, the traps would remain fundamentally the same.

'Why haven't you tried to attack before this?'

'I have,' Red Orc replied. 'Several times. My men got into the house, but I never saw them again. The last attempt was made about three years ago.

'If you don't succeed,' Orc continued, 'I will threaten Urthona with the Beller. I doubt, however, that that will do much good, since he will find it inconceivable that a Lord could do such a thing.'

His tone also made it evident that he did not think Kickaha would succeed.

He wanted to know Kickaha's plans, but Kickaha could only tell him that he had none except to improvise. He wanted Orc to use his devices to ensure a minute's distortion of Urthona's detection devices.

Orc objected to loaning Kickaha an antigravity belt. What if it fell into the hands of the Earthlings?

'There's not much chance of that,' Kickaha said. 'Once I'm in Urthona's territory, I'll either succeed or fail. In either case, the belt isn't going to get into any outsider's hands. And if it did, whoever is Lord will have the influence to see that it is taken out of the hands of whoever has it. I'm sure that even if the FBI had it in their possession, the Lord of the Two Earths could find a way to get it from them. Right?'

'Right,' Orc said. 'But do you plan on running away with it instead of attacking Urthona?'

'No. I won't stop until I'm dead, or too incapacitated to fight, or have won,' Kickaha said.

Orc was satisfied, and by this Kickaha knew that the truth drug was still effective. Orc stood up and said, 'I'll prepare things for you. It will take some time, so you might as well rest or do whatever you think best. We'll go into action at midnight tonight.'

Kickaha asked if the cord could be taken off him. Orc said, 'Why not? You can't get out of here, anyway. The cord was just an extra precaution.'

One of the kilted men touched the shackle around his leg with a thin cylinder. The shackle opened and fell off. While the two men backed away from Kickaha, Orc strode out of the room. Then the door was shut, and Kickaha was alone.

He spent the rest of the time thinking, exercising, and eating lunch and supper. Then he bathed and shaved, exercised some more, and lay down to sleep. He would need all his alertness, strength, and quickness and there was no use draining these with worry and sleeplessness.

He did not know how long he had slept. The room was still lighted, and everything seemed as when he had lain down. The tray with its empty plates and cups was still on the table, and this, he realized, was a wrong note. It should have been gated out.

The sounds that had awakened him had seemed to be slight tappings. When coming out of his sleep, he had dreamed, or thought he dreamed, that a woodpecker was rapping a tree trunk.

Now there was only silence.

He rose and walked towards the door used by Orc and his servants. It was of metal, as he had ascertained after being loosed from the cord. He placed his ear against it and listened. He could hear nothing. Then he jumped back with an oath. The metal had suddenly become hot!

The floor trembled as if an earthquake had started. The metal of the door gave forth a series of sounds, and he knew where the dream of the woodpecker had originated. Something was striking the door on the other side.

He stepped away from it just as the centre of the door became cherry red and began to melt. The redness spread, became white, and then the centre disappeared, leaving a hole the size of a dinner plate. By then, Kickaha was crouching behind the sofa and looking out around its corner. He saw an arm reach in through the hole and the hand grope around the side. Evidently it was trying to locate a lock. There was none, so the arm withdrew and a moment later the edge of the door became cherry red. He suspected that a beam was being used on it, and he wondered what the metal was. If it had been the hardest steel, it should have gone up in a puff of smoke at the first touch of a beam.

The door fell inwards with a clang. A man jumped in, a big cylinder with a bell-like muzzle and a rifle-type stock in his hands. The man was one of the kilted servants. But he carried on his back a black bell-like object in a net attached to the shoulders with straps.

Kickaha saw all this in a glance and withdrew his head. He crouched on the other side, hoping that the intruder had not seen him and would not, as a matter of precaution, sweep the sofa with the beamer to determine if anyone would be behind it. He knew who the man *now* was. Whatever he *may* have been, he was now the Black Beller, Thabuuz. The mind of the Beller was housed in the brain of the servant of the Lord, and the mind of the servant was discharged.

Somehow, the Beller had gotten the bell and managed to transfer his mind from the wounded body of the Drachelander to the servant of the Lord. He had gotten hold of a powerful beamer, and he was on his way out of the stronghold of Red Orc.

The odour of burned flesh filled the room; there must be bodies in the next room.

Kickaha wanted desperately to find out what the Beller was doing, but he did not dare to try to peek around the corner of the sofa again. He could hear the man's breathing, and then, suddenly, it was gone. After waiting sixty seconds and hearing nothing, Kickaha peeked around the corner. The room seemed to be empty. A moment later, he was sure of it. The other door, the door by which Kickaha and Orc and his men had originally entered, was standing wide open, its lock drilled through.

Kickaha looked cautiously around the side of the opposite door. There were parts of human bodies here, arms, trunks, a head, all burned deeply. There seemed to have been four or five men originally. There was no way of telling which was Red Orc or if he was among the group, since all clothes and hair had been burned off.

Somewhere, softly, an alarm was ringing.

He was torn between the desire to keep on the trail of the Beller so that he would not lose him and by the desire to find out if Red Orc was still alive. He also wanted very much to confirm his suspicions that he was not on the Earth he knew. He suspected that the door through which he had entered was a gate between the two worlds and that this house was on Earth Number Two.

He went into the hallway. There were some knives on the floor, but they were too hot to pick up. He went down the hall and through a doorway into a very large room. It was dome-shaped, its walls white with frescoes of sea life, its furniture wooden and lightly built with carved motifs he did not recognize, and its floor a mosaic of stone with more representations of sea creatures.

He crossed the room and looked out the window. There was enough light from the moon to see a wide porch with tall round wooden pillars, painted white, and beyond that a rocky beach that sloped for a hundred yards from the house to the sea. There was no one in view.

He prowled the rest of the house, trying to combine caution with speed. He found a hand-beamer built to look like a conventional revolver. Its butt bore markings that were not the writing of the Lords or of any language that he knew. He tested it out against a chair, which fell apart down the middle. He could find no batteries to recharge it and had no way of knowing how much charge remained in the battery.

He also found closets with clothes, most of them kilts, sandals, beads, and jackets with puffed sleeves. But in one closet he found Earth Number One type clothing, and he put on a shirt and trousers too large for him. Since he could not wear the big shoes, he put on a pair of sandals.

Finally, in a large bedroom luxuriously provided with alien furniture, he discovered how Red Orc had escaped. A crescent lay in the centre of the floor. The Lord had stepped into a circle formed of two crescents of a gate and been transported elsewhere. That he had done so to save himself was evident. The door and the walls were criss-crossed with thin perforations and charred. It was not likely that Orc would be caught without a weapon on him, but he must have thought that the big beamer was too much to face.

He had gated, but where? He could have gone back to Earth Number One, but not necessarily to the same house. Or he could have gated to another place on Earth Number Two. Or, even, to another room in this house.

Kickaha had to get out of this house and after the Beller. He ran downstairs, through the big room, down the hall, and into the room where he had been kept prisoner. The door through which the Beller had gone was still open. Kickaha hesitated before it, because the Beller might be waiting for someone to follow. Then it occurred to him that the Beller would think that everybody in the house had fled or gone and that nobody would be following him. He had not known about the other prisoner, of course, or he would have looked around to dispose of him first.

He returned to the hallway. One knife lying on the floor had cooled off by then and seemed to be undamaged. He hefted it, determined that it had a good balance, and stuck it in his belt. He leaped through the doorway, his gun ready if somebody should be waiting for him. There was no one. The short and narrow hallway was quiet. The door beyond had been closed, and he pushed it open gently with the tip of his dagger. After the door had swung open, he waited a minute, listening. Before going through, he inspected the room. It had changed. It was larger, and the grey-blue paper walls were grey smooth stone. He had expected that this might happen. Red Orc would change the resonance of the gates so that if a prisoner did escape, he would find himself in a surprising, and probably unpleasant, place.

Under other circumstances, Kickaha would have turned back and looked for the switch that would set the gate to the frequency he desired. But now his first duty was to those in the hands of Urthona. To hell with the Beller! It would really be best to get back to Earth Number One and to get started on the attack against Urthona.

He turned and started to re-enter the room where he had been held, and again he stopped. That room had changed, though he would not have known it if the door to the opposite side had not been removed by the Beller's weapon. This door looked exactly the same, but it was upright and in place. Only this kept Kickaha from stepping into it and so finding himself gated to another place where he would be cut off from both the Beller and Urthona's captives.

He set his teeth together and hissed rage and frustration. Now he could do nothing but take second-best and put himself in with the Beller and hope that he could figure a way out.

He turned and went back through the door after the Beller, though no less cautiously.

This room seemed to be safe, but the room beyond that would probably tell him where he was. However, it was just like the one he had left except that there were some black metal boxes, each about six feet square, piled along the walls almost to the ceiilng. There were no locks or devices on them to indicate how they were opened.

He opened the next door slowly, looked through, and then leaped in. He was in a large room furnished with chairs, divans, tables, and statuary. A big fountain was in the middle. The furniture looked as if it had been made by a Lord; though he did not know the name of the particular style, he recognized it. Part of the ceiling and one side of the right wall were curved and transparent. The ground was not visible for some distance and then it abruptly sprang into view. It sloped down for a thousand feet to end in a valley which ran straight and level for several miles and then became the side of a small mountain.

It was daylight outside, but the light was pale, though it was noon. The sun was smaller than Earth's, and the sky was black. The earth itself was rocky with some stretches of reddish sand, and there were a few widely separated cactus-looking plants on the slope and in the valley. They seemed small, but he realized after a while that they must be enormous.

He examined the room carefully and made sure that the door to the next room was closed. Then he looked through the window again. The scene was desolate and eerie. Nothing moved, and probably nothing had moved here for thousands of years. Or so it seemed to him. He could see past the end of the mountain on which the building stood and the end of the other mountain. The horizon was closer than it should have been.

He had no idea where he was. If he had been gated into another universe, he would probably never know. If he had been gated to another planet in his native universe, or its double, then he was probably on Mars. The size of the sun, the reddish sand, the distance of the horizon, the fact that there was enough air to support plant life – if that was plant life – and, even as he watched, the appearance of a swift whitish body coming from the western sky indicated that this was Mars.

For all he knew, this building had been on Mars for fifteen thousand years, since the creation of this universe.

At that moment, something came flapping over the mountain on the opposite side and then glided towards the bottom of the valley. It had an estimated wing span of fifty yards and looked like a cross between a kite, a pterodactyl, and a balloon. Its wingbones gave the impression of being thin as tin foil, though it was really impossible to be sure at that distance. The skin of the wings looked thinner than tissue paper. Its body was a great sac which gave the impression, again unverifiable, of containing gas. Its tail spread out in a curious configuration like six box kites on a rod. Its lower limbs were exceedingly thin but numerous and spread out below it like a complicated landing gear, which it probably was. Its feet were wide and many-toed.

It glided down very gracefully and swiftly. Even with the lift of its great wings and tail and the lighter-than-air aspect of the swollen gas-containing body, it had to glide at a steep angle. The air must be so thin.

The thing threw an enormous shadow over one of the gigantic cactusoids, and then it was settling down, like a skyscraper falling, on the plant. Red dust flew into the air and came down more swiftly than it would have on Earth.

The plant was completely hidden under the monster's bulk. It thrust its rapier-like beak down between two of its legs and, presumably, into the plant. And there it squatted, as motionless as the cactusoids.

Kickaha watched it until it occurred to him that the Beller might also be watching it. If this were so, it would make it easier for Kickaha to surprise him. He went through the next door in the same manner as the last and found himself in a room ten times as large as the one he had just left. It was filled with great metal boxes and consoles with many screens and instruments. It, too, had a window with a view of the valley.

There was no Beller, however.

Kickaha went into the next room. This was small and

furnished with everything a man would need except human companionship. In the middle of the floor lay a skeleton.

There was no evidence of the manner of death. The skeleton was that of a large male. The teeth were in perfect condition. It lay on its back with both bony arms outstretched.

Kickaha thought that it must have been some Lord who had either entered this fortress on Mars from a gate in some other universe or had been trapped elsewhere and transported here by Red Orc. This could have happened ten thousand years ago or fifty years ago.

Kickaha picked the skull up and carried it in his left hand. He might need something to throw as a weapon or as a distraction to his enemy. It amused him to think of using a long-dead lord, a failed predecessor, against a Beller.

The next room was designed like a grotto. There was a pool of water about sixty yards wide and three hundred long in the centre and a small waterfall on the left which came down from the top of a granite cone. There were several of the stone cones and small hills, strange looking plants growing here and there, a tiny stream flowing from a spring on top of another cone, and huge lilypad-like plants in the pool.

As he walked slowly along the wet and slimy edge of the pool, he was startled by a reddish body leaping from a lily pad. It soared out, its legs trailing behind frog-fashion and then splashed into the water. It arose a moment later and turned to face the man. Its face was frog-like but its eyes were periscopes of bone or cartilage. Its pebbly skin was as red as the dust on the surface outside.

There were several shadowy fish-like bodies in the depths. There had to be something for the frog to eat, and for the prey of the frog to eat. The ecology in this tiny room must be delicately but successfully balanced. He doubted that Red Orc came here very often to check up on it.

He was standing by the edge of the pool when he saw the door at the far end begin to open. He had no time to run forward or backward because of the distance he would have to traverse. There was no hiding place to his right and only the pool close by on his left. Without more than a second's pause, he chose the pool and slid over the slimy edge into the water. It was warm enough not to shock him but felt oily. He stuck the beamer in his belt and, still holding the skull in one hand, submerged with a shove of his sandalled feet against the side of the pool. He went down deep, past the thick stems of the lilypads, and swam as far as he could under the water. When he came up, he did so slowly and alongside the stem of a lily. Emerging, he kept his head under the pad of the plant and hoped that the Beller would not notice the bulge. The other rooms had been bright with the equal-intensity, hidden-source lighting of the Lords. But this room was lit only by the light from the window and so had a twilight atmosphere on this side.

Kickaha clung with one hand to the stem of the plant and peered out from under the lifted edge of the pad. What he saw almost made him gasp. He was fortunate to have restrained himself, because his mouth was under water.

The black bell was floating along the edge of the pool at a height of about seven feet above the floor.

It went by slowly and then stopped at the door. A moment later, the Beller entered and walked confidently towards it.

Kickaha began to get some idea of what had happened in Red Orc's house.

The Beller, while in the laboratories of Wolff, must have equipped his bell with an antigravity device. And he must have added some device for controlling it at a distance with his thoughts. He had not been able to use it while on Earth nor had any reason to do so until he was taken prisoner by Orc. Then, when he had recovered enough from the wound, he saw his chance and summoned the bell to him with his thoughts. Or, to be more exact, by controlled patterns of brainwaves which could be detected by the bell. the control must be rough and limited, but it had been effective enough.

Somehow, the bell, operating at the command of the Beller's brainwave patterns, had released him. And the Beller had seized one of Orc's men, discharged the neural pattern of the man's mind, and transferred his mind from the wounded body of Thabuuz to the brain of the servant.

The bell could detect the mental call of the Beller when it extended the two tiny drill-antennas from two holes in its base. The stuff of which the bell was made was indestructible, impervious even to radiation. So the antennas must have come out automatically at certain intervals to 'listen' for the brainwaves of the Beller. And it had 'heard' and had responded. And the Beller had gotten out and obtained a weapon and started to kill. He had succeeded; he may even have killed Red Orc, though Kickaha did not think so.

And then he had been shunted through the escape gate into a building on Mars.

Kickaha watched the Beller approach. Unable to hang onto the skull any longer and handle his gun at the same time, he let the skull drop. It sank silently into the depths while he held onto the stem with his left hand and pulled the beamer from his belt with the other. The Beller went on by him and then stopped at the door. After opening this, he waited until the bell had floated on through ahead of him.

Apparently, the bell could detect other living beings, too. Its range must be limited, otherwise it would have detected Kickaha in the water as it went by. It was possible, of course, that the water and the lilypad shielded him from the bell's probe.

Kickaha pulled himself higher out of the water with his left hand and lifted the beamer above the surface. From under the darkness of the pad, he aimed at the Beller. It would be necessary to get him with the first beam. If it missed, the Beller would get through the door and then Kickaha would be up against a weapon much more powerful than his.

If he missed the Beller, the beam would slice through the wall of the building, and the air would boil out into the thin atmosphere of Mars. And both of them would have had it.

The Beller was presenting his profile. Kickaha held his beamer steadily as he pointed it so that the thread-thin ray would burn a hole through the hip of the man. And then, as he fell, he would be cut in two.

His finger started to squeeze on the trigger. Suddenly, something touched his calf and he opened his mouth to scream. So intense was the pain, it almost shocked him into unconsciousness. He doubled over, and water entered his mouth and nostrils, and he choked. His hand came loose from the plant stem and the beamer fell from the other hand.

In the light-filled water, he saw a frog-like creature swim away swiftly, and he knew that it was this that had bitten him. He swam upwards because he had to get air, knowing even as he did that the Beller would easily kill him, if the Beller had heard him.

He came up and, with a massive effort of will, kept himself from blowing out water and air and gasping and thrashing around. His head came up under the pad again, and he eased the water out. He saw that the Beller had disappeared.

But in the next second he doubled over again with agony. The frog had returned and bitten him on the leg again. His blood poured out from the wounds and darkened the water. He swam quickly to the edge of the pool and pulled himself out with a single smooth motion. His legs tingled.

On the walk, he pulled off his shirt and tore it into strips to bind around his wounds. The animal must have had teeth as sharp as a shark's; they had sheared through the cloth of his pants and taken out skin and flesh. But the wounds were not deep.

The Lord must have been greatly amused when he planted the savage little carnivore in this pool.

Kickaha was not amused. He did not know why the Beller was in the next room, but he suspected that he would soon be back. He had to get away, but he also needed his beamer. Not that he would be able to get it. Not while that frog-thing was in the pool.

At least he had the knife. He took it from his belt and put it between his teeth while he splashed water on the walk where his blood had dripped. Then he straightened up and limped past the pool and into the next room.

He passed through a short bare-walled hall. The room beyond was as large as the one with the pool. It was warm and humid and filled with plant life that looked neither Terrestrial nor Martian. It was true that he had not seen any Martian vegetation other than the cactusoids in the valley. But these plants were so tall, green, stinking, fleshy, and so active, they just did not look as if they could survive on the rare-aired Mars-scape.

One side of the wall was transparent, and this showed a grey fog. That was all. Strain his eyes as much as he could, he could see nothing but the greyness. And it did not seem to be a watery fog but one composed of thousands upon thousands of exceedingly tiny particles. More like dust of some kind, he thought.

He was surely no longer on Mars. When he had passed from the hall into this room, he had stepped through a gate which had shot him instantaneously into a building on some other planet or satellite. The gravity seemed no different than Earth's so he must be on a planet of similar size. That, plus the cloud, made him think that it must be Venus.

With a start, he realized that the gravity in the Martian building should have been much less than Earth's. how much? A sixth? He did not remember, but he knew that when he had leaped, he should have soared far more than he did.

But that building was on Mars. He was sure of that. This meant that the building had been equipped with a device to ensure an Earth-gravity locally. Which meant that this building could be on, say, Jupiter, and yet the titanic drag of the planet would be nullified by the Lord's machines.

He shrugged. It really did not matter much where he was if he could not survive outside of the building. The problem he had to solve was staying alive and finding a way back to Earth. He went on to another short and bare hall and then into a twilit room the size of Grand Central Station. It was dome-shaped and filled with a silvery grey metal liquid except for a narrow walk around the wall and for a small round island in the middle. The metal looked like mercury, and the walk went all the way around the room. Nowhere along the wall was there any sign of any opening.

The island was about fifty yards from the wall. Its surface was only a foot above the still lake of quicksilver. The island seemed to be of stone, and in its exact centre was a huge hoop of metal set vertically in the stone. He knew at once that it was a gate and that if he could get to it, he would be transported to a place where he would at least have a fighting chance. That was the rule of the game. If the prisoner was intelligent enough and strong enough and swift enough – and, above all, lucky enough – he just might get free.

He waited by the door because there was no other place to hide. While he waited, he tried to think of anything in the other rooms that could be converted to a boat. Nothing came to his mind except one of the sofas, and he doubted that it would float. Still, he might try it. But how did you propel a heavy object that was slowly sinking, or perhaps swiftly sinking, through mercury?

He would not know until he tried it. The thought did not cheer him up. And then he thought, could a man swim in mercury? In addition, there were poisonous vapours rising from mercury, if he remembered his chemistry correctly.

Now he remembered some phrases from his high school chemistry class. That was back in 1936 in a long ago and truly different world: *Does not wet glass but forms a convex surface when in a glass container ... is slightly volatile at ordinary temperatures and a health hazard due to its poisonous effect ... slowly tarnishes in moist air...*

The air in this dome was certainly moist, but the metal was not tarnished. And he could smell no fumes and did not feel any poisonous effects. Not as yet.

Suddenly, he stiffened. He heard, faintly, the slapping of leather on stone. The door had been left open by the Beller, so Kickaha had not moved it. He was on the other side, waiting, hoping that the bell would not enter first.

It did. The black object floated through about four feet off the floor. As soon as it had passed by, it stopped. Kickaha leaped against the door and slammed it shut. The bell continued to hover in the same spot.

The door remained shut. It had no lock, and all the Beller had to do to open it was to kick it. But he was cautious, and he must have been very shaken by finding the door closed. He had no idea who was on the other side or what weapons his enemy had. Furthermore, he was now separated from his bell, his most precious possession. If it was true that the bell could not be destroyed, it was also true that it could be taken away and hidden from him.

Kickaha ran in front of the door, hoping that the Beller would not fire his heavy beamer at it at that moment. He seized the bell in his hands and plunged on. The bell resisted but went backwards all the same. It did not, however, give an inch on the vertical.

At that moment, the metal of the edge of the door and the wall began to turn red, and Kickaha knew that the Beller was turning the full power of his beamer on the door and that the metal must be very resistant indeed.

But why didn't the Beller just kick the door open and then fire through it?

Perhaps he was afraid that his enemy might be hiding behind the door when it swung open, so he was making sure that there would be nothing to swing. Whatever his motives, he was giving Kickaha a little more time, not enough though to swim across to the island. The Beller would be through the door about the time he was halfway to the island.

Kickaha took hold of the bell with both hands and pushed it up against the wall. It did not go easily on the horizontal, but he did not have to strain to move it. He pulled it towards him and then away, estimating its resistance. Then he gave it a great shove with both hands in the direction along the wall. It moved at about two feet per second but then slowed as it scraped along the curved wall. Another shove, this time at an angle to take it away from the curve but to keep it from going out over the pool, resulted in its moving for a longer distance.

He looked at the door. The red spot was a hole now with a line of redness below it. Evidently the Beller intended to carve out a large hole or perhaps to cut out the door entirely. He could stop at any moment to peek through the hole, and, if he did, he would see his enemy and the bell. On the other hand, he might be afraid to use the hole just yet because his enemy might be waiting to blast him. Kickaha had one advantage. The Beller did not know what weapons he had.

Kickaha hurried after the bell, seized it again, backed up, stopped at the wall, and then drew his feet up. He hung with his knees and toes almost touching the walk. But the bell did not lose a fraction of altitude.

'Here goes everything!' he said and shoved with all the power of his legs against the wall.

He and the bell shot out over the pool, straight towards the vertical hoop on the island. They went perhaps forty feet and then stopped. He looked down at the grey liquid below and slowly extended his feet until they were in the metal. He pushed against it, and it gave way to his feet, but he and the bell moved forward a few feet. And so he pushed steadily and made progress, though it was slow and the sweat poured out over his body and ran into his eyes and stung them and his legs began to ache as if he had run two miles as fast as he could.

Nevertheless, he got to the island, and he stood upon its stone surface with the hoop towering only a few feet from him. He looked at the door. A thin line ran down one side and across the bottom and up the other side. It curved suddenly and was running across the top of the door. Within a minute or two, the door would fall in and then the Beller would come through.

Kickaha looked back through the hoop. The room was visible on the other side, but he knew that if he stepped through it, he would be gated to some other place, perhaps to another universe. Unless the Lord had set it here for a joke.

He pushed the bell ahead of him and then threw himself to one side so he would not be in front of the hoop. He had had enough experience with the Lords to suspect that the place on the other side was trapped. It was always best to throw something into the trap to spring it.

There was a blast that deafened him. His face and the side of his body were seared with heat. He had shut his eyes, but light flooded them. And then he sat up and opened them in time to see the bell shooting across the pool, though still at its original height. It sped above the mercury pool and the walk and stopped only when it slammed into the wall. There it remained, a few inches from the wall because of its rebound.

Immediately thereafter, the door fell outward and down against the walk. He could not hear it; he could hear only the ringing in his ears from the blast. But he saw the Beller dive through the beamer held close to him, hit the floor, roll, and come up with the beamer held ready. By then, Kickaha had jumped up. As he saw the Beller look around and suddenly observe him, he leaped through the hoop. He had no choice. He did not think it would be triggered again, since that was not the way the Lords arranged their traps. But if the trap on the other side was reset, it would blow him apart, and his worries would be over.

He was through, and he was falling. There were several thousands of feet of air beneath him, a blue sky above, and a thin horizontal bar just before him. He grabbed it, both hands clamping around smooth cold iron, and he was swinging at arm's length below a bar, the ends of which were set in two metal poles that extended about twenty feet out from a cliff.

It was a triumph of imagination and sadism for Red Orc. If the prisoner was careless enough to go through the hoop without sending in a decoy, he would be blown apart before he could fall to death. And if he did not jump, but stepped through the gate, he would miss the bar.

And, having caught the bar, then what?

A man with lesser nerve or muscle might have fallen. Kickaha did not waste any time. He reached out with one hand and gripped the support bar. And as quickly let loose while he cursed and swung briefly with one hand.

The support pole was almost too hot to touch.

He inched along the bar to the other support pole and touched it. That was just as hot.

The metal was not quite too hot to handle. It pained him so much that Kickaha thought about letting go. But he stuck to it, and finally, hurting so much that tears came to his eyes and he groaned, he pulled himself up over the lip of the cliff. For a minute he lay on the rock ledge and moaned. The palms of his hands and the inner sides of his fingers felt as if they had third-degree burns. They looked, however, as if they had only been briefly near a fire, not in it, and the pain quickly went away.

His investigation of his situation was short because there was not much to see. He was on the bare top of a pillar of hard black rock. The top was wider than the bottom, and the sides were smooth as the barrel of a cannon. All around the pillar, as far as he could see, was a desolate rock plain and a river. The river split the circle described by the horizon and then itself split when it came to the column. On the other side, it merged into itself and continued on towards the horizon.

The sky was blue, and the yellow sun was at its zenith.

Set around the pillar near its base, at each of the cardinal points of the compass, was a gigantic hoop. One of these meant his escape to a place where he might survive if he chose the right one. The others probably meant certain death if he went through them.

They were not an immediate concern. He had to get down off the pillar first, and at the moment he did not know how he was going to do that.

He returned to the bar projecting from the cliff. The Beller could be about ready to come through the gate. Even if he was reluctant, he would have to come through. This was the only way out.

Minutes passed and became an hour, if he could trust

his sense of time. The sun curved down from the zenith. He walked back and forth to loosen his muscles and speed the blood in his legs and buttocks. Suddenly a foot and a leg came out of the blue air. The Beller, on the other side of the gate, was testing out the unknown.

The foot reached here and there for substance and found only air. It withdrew, and, a few seconds later, the face of the Beller, like a Cheshire Cat in reverse, appeared out of the air.

Kickaha's knife was a streak of silver shooting towards the face. The face jerked back into the nothingness, and the knife was swallowed by the sky at a point about a foot below where the face had been.

The gate was not one-way. The entrance of the knife showed that. The fact that the Beller could stick part of his body through it and then withdraw it did not have anything to do with the one-way nature of some gates. Even a one-way gate permitted a body to go halfway through and then return. Unless, of course, the Lord who had designed it wished to sever the body of the user.

Several seconds passed. Kickaha cursed. He might never find out if he had thrown true or not.

Abruptly, a head shot out of the blue and was followed by a neck and shoulders and a chest and a solar plexus from which the handle of the knife stuck out.

The rest of the body came in view as the Beller toppled through. He fell through and out and his body became smaller and smaller and then was lost in distance. But Kickaha was able to see the white splash it made as it struck the river.

He took a deep breath and sat down, trembling. The Beller was at last dead, and all the universes were safe forever from his kind.

And here I am, Kickaha thought. *Probably the only living thing in this universe. As alone as a man can be. And if I don't think of something impossible to do before my nonexistent breakfast, I will soon be one of the only two dead things in this universe.*

He breathed deeply again and then did what he had to do,

It hurt just as much going back out on the pole as it had coming in. When he reached the bar, he rested on it with one arm and one leg over it. After the pain had gone away in his hands and legs, he swung up onto the bar and balanced himself standing on it. His thousands of hours of practising on tightwires and climbing to great heights paid off. He was able to maintain his equilibrium on the bar while he estimated again the point through which the Beller had fallen. It was only an undefined piece of blue, and he had one chance to hit his target.

He leaped outwards and up, and his head came through the hoop and the upper part of his body and then he went 'Whoof!' as his belly struck on the edge of the hoop. He reached out and gripped the stone with his fingertips and pulled himself on through. For a while, he lay on the stone until his heart resumed its normal beat. He saw that the bell was above him and the beamer was on the floor of the island only a foot from him.

He rose and examined the bell. It was indestructible, and the tips of the antennas were encased in the same indestructible stuff. When the antennas were withdrawn, the tips plugged up the two tiny holes at the base of the bell. But the antennas themselves were made of less durable metal, and they had suffered damage from the blast. Or so he supposed. He could see no damage. In fact, he could not even see the antennas, they were so thin, though he could feel them. But the fact that the Beller had not sent the bell ahead through the gate proved to Kickaha that something had damaged the bell. Perhaps the blast had only momentarily impaired the relatively delicate brainwave and flight-governing apparatus inside the bell. This was, after all, something new, something which the Beller had not had time to field-test.

Whatever had happened, it was fixed at its altitude above the island. And it still put up a weak resistance against a horizontal push.

Kickaha presumed that its antennas must still be operative to some degree. Otherwise, the bell would not know how to maintain a constant height from the ground.

It gave him his only chance to get to the ground several thousand feet below. He did not know how much of a chance. It might just stay at this level even if the ground beneath it were to suddenly drop away. If that happened, he still might be able to get to the top of the stone pillar.

He put the strap of the beamer over one shoulder hugged the bell to his chest, and stepped out through the hoop.

His descent was as swift as if he were dangling at the end of a parachute, a speed better than he had hoped for. From time to time, he had to kick against the sides of the pillar because the bell kept drifting back towards it, as if the mass of the pillar had some attraction for it.

Then he was ten feet above the river and released his hold on the bell. He fell a little faster, hit the water, which was warm, and came up in a strong current. He had to fight to get to shore but managed it. After he had regained some of his strength, he walked along the shore until he saw the bell. It was stopped against the side of the pillar, like a baby beast nuzzling its gigantic mother. There was no way for him to get to it nor did he see any reason why he should.

A few yards on, he found the body of the Beller. It had come to rest against a reef of rock which barely protruded above the surface of the small bay. Its back was split open, and the back of the head was soft, as if it had struck concrete instead of water. The knife was still in its solar plexus. Kickaha pulled it out, and cleaned it on the wet hair of the Beller. The fall had not damaged the knife.

He pulled the body from the river. Then he considered the giant gates set hoop-like in the rock like the smaller one in the island in that other world. Two were on this side of the river and two on the other. Each was at the corner of a square two miles long. He walked to the nearest one and threw a stone into it. The stone went through and landed on the rock on the other side. It was one of Red Orc's jokes. Perhaps all four were just hoops and he would be stuck on this barren world until he starved to death.

The next hoop, in the northeast corner also proved to be just that, a hoop.

Kickaha was beginning to get tired and hungry. He now had to swim over the river, through a very strong current, to get to the other two hoops. The walk from one to the other was two miles, and if he had to test all four, he would walk eight miles. Ordinarily, he would not have minded that at all, but he had been through much in the past few hours.

He sat down for a minute and then he jumped up, exclaiming and cursing himself for a fool. He had forgotten that gates might work when entered in one direction but not work in the other. Picking up a stone, he went around to the other side of the big hoop and cast the stone through it. The hoop was still just a hoop.

There was nothing to do then but to walk back to the first hoop and to test that from the other side. It, too, gave evidence that it was no gate.

He swam the river and got to the other side after having been carried downstream for a half-mile, thus adding to his journey. The beamer made the swimming and the walking more difficult, since it weighed about thirty pounds. But he did not want to leave it behind.

The southwest hoop was only a huge round of metal. He went towards the last one while the sun continued westward and downward. It shone in a silent sky over a silent earth. Even the wind had died down, and the only sound was the rushing of the river, which died as he walked away from it, and his own feet on the rocks and his breathing.

When he got to the northwest hoop, he felt like putting off his rock-throwing for a while. If this proved to be another jest of Red Orc, it might also prove to be the last jest that Kickaha would ever know. So he might as well get this over with.

The first stone went through and struck the rock beyond.

The second went through the other side and fell on the ground beyond.

He jumped up and down and yelled his frustration and hit the palm of one hand with the fist of the other. He kicked at a small boulder and then went howling and hopping away with pain. He pulled his hair and slapped the side of his head and then turned his face towards the blind blue sky and the deaf bright yellow sun and howled like a wolf whose tail was caught in a bear trap.

After a while he became silent and still. He might as well have been made of the light-red rock which was so abundant on this earth, except that his eyelids jumped and his chest rose and fell.

When he broke loose from the mould of contemplation, he walked briskly but unemotionally to the river. Here he drank his fill and then he looked for a sheltered place to spend the night. After fifteen minutes, he found a hollow in the side of a small hill of hard rock that would protect him from the wind. He fell asleep after many unavoidable thoughts of the future.

In the morning, he looked at the Beller's body and wondered if he was going to have to eat it.

To give himself something to do, and also because he never entirely gave up hope or quit trying, he waded around in the shallows of the river and ran his hands through the waters. No fish were touched or scared into revealing their presence. It did not seem likely that there would be any, especially when there was an absolute absence of plant life.

He walked to the top of the hill in the base of which he had slept. He sat on the hard round peak for a while, moving only to ease the discomfort of the stone on his buttocks. His situation was desperate and simple. Either Red Orc had prepared a way for his prisoner to escape if he was clever and agile enough or he had not. If he had not, then the prisoner would die here. If he had, then the prisoner – in this case, Kickaha – was just not bright enough. In which case, the prisoner was going to die soon.

He sat for a long while and then he groaned. What was the matter with his brain? Sure, the stone had gone through the gates, but no flesh had passed through them. He should have tried them himself instead of trickily testing them only with the stones. The gates could be set up to trigger only if matter above a certain mass passed through them or sometimes only if protein passed through them. Or even only if human brainwaves came close enough to set them off. But he had been so concerned with traps on the other side that he had forgotten about this possibility.

However, any activated gate might be adjusted to destroy the first large mass that entered, just as the gate from the room with the mercury pool had been booby-trapped.

He groaned at the thought of the strain and sweat involved, but he had not survived thus far by being lazy. He lifted the body of the Beller onto his shoulder, thanking his fortunes that the man was small, and set off towards the nearest gate.

It was a long, hot, and muscle-trembling day. The lack of food weakened him, and every failure at each gate took more out of him. The swim across the river with the dead weight of the corpse and the beamer drained him of even more. But he cast the body six times through the three gates, once through each side.

And now he was resting beside the fourth. The Beller lay near him, its arms spread out, its face upturned to the hot sun, its eyes open, its mouth open, and a faint odour of corruption rising like invisible flies from it. At least, there were no real flies in this world.

Time passed. He did not feel much stronger. He had to get up and throw the body through both sides. Just rolling it through was out of the question because he did not want to stand in the path of any explosion. It was necessary to stand by the edge of the hoop, lift the body up and throw it through and then leap to one side.

For the seventh time, he did so. The body went through the hoop and sprawled on the ground. He had one last chance, and this time, instead of resting, he picked up the corpse and lifted it up before him until it was chest-high and heaved.

When he raised his head up from his position on the rock, he saw that the body was still visible.

So much for that theory. And so much for him. He was done for.

He sat up instead of just lying there with his eyes closed. This move, made for no motive of which he was aware, saved his life.

Even so, he almost lost it. The tigerish beast that was charging silently over the hard rock roared when it saw him sit up and increased the lengths of its bounds and its speed. Kickaha was so surprised that he froze for a second and thus gave the animal an edge. But he did not give enough. The beamer fired just as the animal rose for its final arc, and the ray bored through its head, sliced it, cut through the neck and chest, took off part of a leg, and drilled into the rock beyond. The body struck the ground and slid into him and knocked him off his feet and rolled him over and over. He hurt in his legs and his back and chest and hands and nose when he arose. Much skin had been burned off by his scraping against the rock, and where the body of the beast had slammed into his legs was a dull pain that was to get sharper.

Nevertheless, the animal looked edible. And he thought he knew where it had come from. After he had cut off several steaks and cooked and eaten them, he would return to the northwest gate and investigate again.

The beast was about a quarter larger than a Siberian tiger, had a cat-like build, thick long fur with a tawny undercoat and pale red zigzag stripes on head and body and black stocking-like fur on the lower part of the legs and the paws. Its eyes were lemonade-yellow, and its teeth were more those of a shark's than a cat's.

The steaks tasted rank, but they filled him with strength. He took the Beller by the arm and dragged him the two miles to the gate. The corpse, by this time, was in a badly damaged condition. It stank even stronger when he lifted it up and threw it through the gate.

This time, it disappeared, and it was followed by a spurt of oil from the gate that would have covered him if he had been standing directly before it within a range of ten yards. Immediately after, the oily substance caught fire and burned for fifteen minutes.

Kickaha waited until long after the fire was out and then

he jumped through with his beamer ready. He did not know what to expect. There might be another of the tigers waiting for him. It was evident that the first time he had thrown the Beller through it, he had set off a delaying activation which had released the beast through it some time after he had given up on it. It was a very clever and sadistic device and just the sort of thing he could expect from Red Orc. It seemed to him, however, that Red Orc might have given up setting any more machines. He would believe that it was very unlikely that anybody could have gotten this far.

For a second, he was in a small bare room with a large cage, its door open, and a black dome on three short legs. Then, he was in another room. This one was larger and was made of some hard grey metal or plastic and lacked any decoration and had no furniture except a seatless commode, a washbowl and a single faucet, and a small metal table fastened to the floor with chains.

The transition from one room to the other shocked him, although he could explain how it happened. On jumping through the hoop into this room, he had triggered a delayed gate. This, activated, had sent him into this seemingly blind-alley chamber.

The light had no visible source; it filled the room with equal intensity. It was bright enough so that he could see that there were no cracks or flaws in the walls. There was nothing to indicate a window or door. And the walls were made of sturdy stuff. The ray from the beamer, turned to full power, only warmed the wall and the air in the chamber. He turned the weapon off and looked for the source of air, if there was one.

After an extensive inspection, he determined that fresh air moved in slowly from a point just above the table top. This meant that it was being gated in through a device embedded inside the solid table top. And the air moved out through another gate that had to be embedded in the wall in an upper corner of wall and ceiling. The gates would be operating intermittently and were set for admission only of gases.

He turned the full power of the beamer on the table top, but that was as resistant as the walls. However, unless his captor intended him to starve, he would have provided a gate through which to transmit food to his captive. It probably would be the same gate as that in the table top, but when the time came for the meal, the gate would be automatically set for passage of solid material.

Kickaha considered this for a while and wondered why no one had thought of this idea for escape. Perhaps the Lord had thought of it and was hoping that his prisoner also would. It would be just the kind of joke a Lord would enjoy. Still, it was such a wild idea, it might not have occurred to the Lord.

He imagined that alarms must be flashing and sounding somewhere in the building which housed this chamber. That is, if the chamber was in a building and not in some deserted pocket universe. If, however, the Lord should be away, then he might return too late to keep his prisoner imprisoned.

He had no exact idea of how much time passed, but he estimated that it was about four hours later when the tray appeared on the table. It held Earth food, a steak medium well-done, a salad of lettuce, carrots, onions, and a garlic dressing, three pieces of brown European bread with genuine butter, and a dish of chocolate ice cream.

He felt much better when he finished, indeed, almost grateful to his captor. He did not waste any time after swallowing the last spoonful of ice cream, however. He climbed onto the top of the table, the beamer held on his shoulder with the strap, and the tray in his hands. He then bent over and, balancing on one leg, set the tray down and then stepped onto it. He reasoned that the gate might be activated by the tray and dishes and not by a certain mass. He was betting his life that the influence of the gate would extend upwards enough to include him in it. If it did not, somebody on the other end was going to be surprised by half a corpse. If it did, somebody was still going to be surprised and even more unpleasantly.

Suddenly, he was on a table inside a closet lit by one

overhead light. If he had not been crouching, he would have been deprived of his head by the ceiling as he materialized.

He got down off the table and swung the door open and stepped out into a very large kitchen. A man was standing with his back to him, but he must have heard the door moving because he wheeled around. His mouth was open, his eyes were wide, and he said, 'What the . . .?'

Kickaha's foot caught him on the point of the chin, and he fell backwards, unconscious, onto the floor. After listening to make sure that the noise of the man's fall had not disturbed anyone, Kickaha searched the man's clothes.

He came up with a sawed-off Smith & Wesson .38 in a shoulder holster and a wallet with a hundred and ten dolars in bills, two driver's licences, the omnipresent credit cards, and a business card. The man's name was Robert di Angelo.

Kickaha put the gun in his belt after checking it and then inspected the kitchen. It was so large that it had to be in a mansion of a wealthy man. He quickly found a small control board behind a sliding panel in the wall which was half open. Several lights were blinking on it.

The fact that di Angelo had sent down a meal to him showed that the dwellers of this house knew they had a prisoner. Or, at least, that the Lord knew it. His men might not be cognizant of gates, but they would have been told to report to Red Orc if the lights on this panel and others flashed out and, undoubtedly, sound alarms were activated. The latter would have been turned off by now, of course.

There must be a visual monitor of the prison, so the Lord, Urthona, in this case, must know whom he held. Why hadn't Urthona at once taken steps to question his captive? He must surely be burning to know how Kickaha had gotten in there.

He ran water into a glass and dashed it in the face of the man on the floor. Di Angelo started and rolled his head and his eyes opened. He jerked again when he saw Kickaha over him and felt the point of the knife at his throat.

'Where is your boss?' Kickaha said.

Di Angelo said, 'I don't know.'

'Ignorance isn't bliss in your case,' Kickaha said. He pushed the knife in so that blood trickled out from the side of the neck.

The man's eyes widened, and he said, 'Take it easy,' and then, 'What difference does it make? You haven't got a chance. Here's what happened . . .'

Di Angelo was the cook, but he was also aware of what was going on in the lower echelons. He had been told long ago to inform the boss, whom he called Mr. Callister, if the alarms were activated in the kitchen. Until tonight, they had been dormant. When they did go off, startling him, he had called Mr. Callister, who was with his gang on business di Angelo knew nothing about. It must have something to do with the recent troubles, those that had come with the appearance of Kickaha and the others. Callister had told him what to do, which was only to prepare a meal, set it on the table in the closet, close the closet door, and press a button on the control panel.

Kickaha asked about Wolff, Chryseis, and Anana. Di Angelo said, 'Some of the guys took them into the boss' office and left them there and that's the last anybody's seen of them. Honest to God, I'm telling the truth! If anybody knows where they went, it's Callister. Him and him only!'

Kickaha made di Angelo get up and lead him through the house. They went through some halls and large rooms, all luxuriously furnished, and then up a broad winding marble staircase to the second floor. On the way, di Angelo told him that this house was in a walled estate in Beverly Hills. The address was that which Red Orc had said was Urthona's.

'Where are the servants?' he said.

'They've either gone home or to their quarters over the garage,' di Angelo said. 'I'm not lying, mister, when I say I'm the only one in the house.'

The door to Callister's office was of heavy steel and locked. Kickaha turned the beamer on it and sliced out the lock with a brief quick rotation of the barrel. Di Angelo's eyes bulged, and he turned paler. Evidently he knew nothing of the weapons of the Lord.

Kickaha found some tape in a huge mahogany desk and taped di Angelo's hands behind him and his ankles together. While di Angelo sat in a chair, Kickaha made a quick but efficient search of the office. The control panel for what he hoped were the gates popped out of a section of the big desk when a button in a corner of the desk was pressed. The pushbuttons, dials, and lights were identified by markings that would have mystified any Earthling but Kickaha. These were in the writing of the Lords.

However, he did not know the nature of Gates Number One through Ten nor what would happen if he pressed a button marked with the symbol for *M*. That could mean many thousands of things, but he suspected that it stood for *miyrtso,* meaning death.

The first difficulty in using the panel was that he did not know where the gates were even if he activated them. The second was that he probably could not activate them. The Lord was not foolish enough to leave an operable system which was also relatively accessible. He would carry on his person some device which had to be turned on before the control panel would be energized. But at least Kickaha knew where the panel was so that if he ever got hold of the activator, he could use the panel. That is, if he also located the gates.

It was very frustrating because he was so sure that Anana and his two friends, if they were still alive, were behind one of the ten gates.

The telephone rang. Kickaha was startled but quickly recovered. He picked up the phone and carried it over to di Angelo and put the receiver at a distance between both their ears. Di Angelo did not need to be told what was expected of him. He said, 'Hello!'

The voice that answered was Ramos'.

'Di Angelo? Just a minute.'

The next voice was that of the man Kickaha had talked to when he thought he was speaking to Red Orc. This must be Urthona, and whatever it was that had brought him out in the open had to be something very important. The only thing that would do that would be a chance to get Red Orc.

'Angelo? I'm getting an alarm transmission here. It's coming from my office. Did you know that?'

Kickaha shook his head and di Angelo said, 'No, sir.'

'Well, someone is in my office. Where are you?'

'In the kitchen, sir,' di Angelo said.

'Get up there and find out what's going on,' Urthona said. 'I'll leave this line open. And I'm sending over men from the warehouse to help you. Don't take any chances. Shoot to kill unless you're dead certain you can get the drop on him. You understand?'

'Yes, sir,' di Angelo said.

The phone clicked. Kickaha did not feel triumphant. Urthona must realize that anyone in the office could have picked up the phone to listen in. He knew this cut down any chance of di Angelo's surprising the intruder and meant that the reinforcements would have to be rushed over as swiftly as possible.

Kickaha taped di Angelo's mouth and locked him in the closet. He then destroyed the control panel for the gates with a flash from the beamer. If Urthona meant to transfer his other prisoners – if he had any – or to do anything to them, he would be stopped for a while. He would have to build another panel – unless he had some duplicates in storage.

His next step was to get out of the house quickly and down to the railroad station, where the Horn was in a locker. He wished that he could have gotten the Horn first, because then he might have been able to use it unhindered. Now, Urthona would be certain to guard his house well.

Kickaha had to leave the house and go downtown. He decided to cache the beamer on the estate grounds. He found a depression in the ground behind a large oleander bush near the wall. The estate was excellently gardened; there were no loose leaves or twigs with which to cover the weapon. He placed it in the depression and left it there. He also decided to leave the gun which he had taken from di Angelo. It was too bulky to conceal under his shirt.

He left without incident except having to return to the beamer's hiding place so he could use it to burn through the lock on the iron gate that was the exit to the street. This was set in a high brick wall with spikes on top. The guardhouse by the big iron gate to the driveway was unoccupied, apparently because Urthona had pulled everybody except di Angelo from the house. There were controls in the guardhouse, and he easily identified those that worked both gates. But the power or the mechanisms had been shut off, and he did not want to take the time to return to the house to question di Angelo. He burned through the lock mechanism and pushed the gate open. Behind him, a siren began whooping and he could see lights flashing on the control board in the guardhouse. If the noise continued, the police would be called in. Kickaha smiled at that thought. Then he lost his smile. He did not want the police interfering any more than Urthona did.

After hiding the beamer behind the bush again, he walked southward. After five blocks, he came to Sunset. He was apprehensive that a police car might notice him, because he understood that any pedestrians in this exclusive and extremely wealthy neighbourhood were likely to be stopped by the police. Especially at night.

But his luck held out, and he was able to hail a taxi. The driver did not want to go that far out of Beverly Hills, but Kickaha opened the back door and got into the car. 'This is an emergency,' he said. 'I got a business appointment which involves a lot of money.'

He leaned forward and handed the driver a twenty-dollar bill from di Angelo's wallet. This is yours, over and above the fare and the regular tip. Think you can detour a little?'

'Can do,' the cabbie said.

He let Kickaha off three blocks from the railroad station, since Kickaha did not want him to know where he was going if the police should question him. He walked to the station, removed the ball of gum and the key from the hollow in the tree, and then went inside the station.

He removed the instrument case from the locker without

interference or attention, other than a four-year-old girl who stared at him with large deep-blue eyes and then said, 'Hello!' He patted her on the head as he went by, causing her mother to pull her away and lecture her in a loud voice about being friendly to strangers.

Kickaha grinned, though he did not really think the incident amusing. During his long years on the World of Tiers, he had become used to children being treated as greatly valued and much-loved beings. Since Wolff had put into the waters of that great world a chemical which gave the humans a thousand-year youth but also cut down considerably on the birth rate, he had ensured that children were valued. There were very few cases of child killings, abuses, or deprivation of love. And while this sort of rearing did not keep the children from growing into adults who were quite savage in warfare – but never killed or maltreated children – it did result in people with much fewer neuroses and psychoses than the civilized Earthlings. Of course, most societies in Wolff's world were rather homogenous, small, and technologically primitive, not subject to the many-levelled crisscross current modes of life of Earth's highly industrial societies.

Kickaha left the station and walked several blocks before coming to a public phone booth in the corner of a large service station area. He dialled Urthona's number. The phone had rung only once when it was picked up and an unfamiliar voice answered. Kickaha said, 'Mr. Callister, please.'

'Who is this?' the rough voice said.

'Di Angelo can describe me,' Kickaha said. 'That is, if you've found him in the closet.'

There was an exclamation and then, 'Just a minute.'

A few seconds later, a voice said, 'Callister speaking.'

'Otherwise known as Urthona, present Lord of Earth,' Kickaha said. 'I am the man who was your prisoner.'

'How did you . . .?' Urthona said and then stopped, realizing that he was not going to get a description of the escape.

'I'm Kickaha,' Kickaha said. There was no harm in identifying himself, since he was sure that Urthona had gotten both his name and description from Anana. 'The Earthling who did what you supposed Lords of Creation could not do. I killed directly, or caused to be killed, all fifty-one of the Bellers. They are no longer a menace. I got out of Red Orc's house in that other Earth, got through all his traps, and got into your house. If you had been there, I would have captured or killed you. Make no mistake about that.

'But I didn't call you just to tell you what I have done. I want only to return in peace to Wolff's world with Wolff, Chryseis, and Anana. You and Red Orc can battle it out here and may the best Lord win. Now that the Beller is dead, there is no reason for us to stay here. Nor for you to keep my friends.'

There was a long silence and then Urthona said, 'How do I know that the Beller is dead?'

Kickaha described what had happened, although he left out several details that he did not think Urthona should know.

'So you now know how you can check out my story,' he said. 'You can't follow my original route as I did, since you don't know where Red Orc's house is, and I don't either. But I think that all the gates are two-way, and you can backtrack, starting from that room in which I ended.'

He could imagine the alternating delight and alarm Urthona was feeling. He now had a route to get into Red Orc's dwelling, but Red Orc could get into his house through that same route, too.

Urthona said, 'You're wrong, I know where Red Orc lives. Did live, that is. One of my men saw him on the street only two hours ago. He thought at first it was me and that I was on some business he'd better keep his nose out of. Then he returned here and saw me and knew I couldn't have gotten here so quickly.

'I realized what good fortune had done for me. I got my men and surrounded the house and we broke in. We had to kill four of his men, but he got away. Gated out, I suppose. And when he did, he eliminated all the gates in the house. There was no way of following him.'

'I had thought that one of the burned corpses might be Red Orc's,' Kickaha said. 'But he is still alive. Well . . .'

'I'm tired of playing this game,' Urthona said. 'I would like to see my brother become one of those charred corpses. I will make a bargain with you again. If you will get Red Orc for me, deliver him to me in a recognizable condition, I will release your friends and guarantee safe passage back to your World of Tiers. That is, if I can satisfy myself that your story about the Beller is true.'

'You know how to do that,' Kickaha said. 'Let me speak to Anana and Wolff, so that I can be sure they're still alive.'

'I can't do that just at this moment,' Urthona said. 'Give me, say, ten minutes. Call back then.'

'Okay,' Kickaha said. He hung up and left the phone booth in a hurry. Urthona might or might not have some means of quickly locating the source of the call, but he did not intend to give him a chance. He hailed a taxi and had it drop him off near the La Brea Tar Pit. From there, he walked up Wilshire until he came to another booth. Fifteen, not ten, minutes had passed. Di Angelo answered the phone this time. Although he must have recognized Kickaha's voice, he said nothing except for him to wait while he switched the call. Urthona's voice was the next.

'You can speak to my niece, the *leblabbiy*-lover, first,' Urthona said.

Anana's lovely voice said, 'Kickaha! Are you all right?'

'Doing fine so far!' Kickaha said. 'The Beller is dead! I killed him myself. And Red Orc is on the run. Hang on. We'll get back to the good world yet. I love you!'

'I love you, too,' she said.

Urthona's voice, savage and sarcastic, cut in. 'Yes, I love you too, *leblabbiy!* Now, do you want to hear from Wolff?'

'I'm not about to take your word that he's O.K.,' Kickaha said.

Wolff's voice, deep and melodious, came over the phone. 'Kickaha, old friend! I knew you'd be along, sooner, or later!'

'Hello, Robert, it's great to hear your voice again! You and Chryseis all right?'

'We're unharmed, yes. What kind of deal are you making with Urthona?'

The Lord said, 'That's enough You satisfied, Earthling?'

'I'm satisfied that they're alive as of this moment,' Kickaha said. 'And they had better be when the moment of payment comes.'

'You don't threaten me!' Urthona said. And then, in a calmer tone, 'Very well. I shall assist you in any way I can. What do you need?'

'The address of Red Orc's house,' Kickaha said.

'Why would you need that?' Urthona said, surprised.

'I have my reasons. What is the address?'

Urthona gave it to him but he spoke slowly as if he were trying to think of Kickaha's reasons for wanting it. Kickaha said, 'That's all I need now. So long.'

He hung up. A minute later, he was in a taxi on his way to Urthona's house. Two blocks away, he paid the driver and walked the rest of the way. The small iron gate was chained now, and the lights in the little guardhouse near the big gate showed three men inside. The mansion was also ablaze, although he could see nobody through the windows.

There did not seem to be any way of getting in just then. He was capable of leaping up and grabbing the top of the wall and pulling himself over, but he did not doubt that there would be alarms on top of the wall. On second thought, so what? At this time, he did not intend to invade the house. All he wanted was to get the beamer and then get out. By the time Urthona's men arrived, he could be back over the wall.

It was first necessary to cache the Horn somewhere, because it would be too awkward, in fact, impossible, to take it with him in scaling the wall. He could throw it over the wall first but did not want to do that. A minute's inspection showed him that he could stick the case in the branches of a bush growing on the strip of grass between the side walk and the street. He returned to the spot by the wall opposite where he had hidden the beamer. He went across the street, stood there a minute waiting until a car went by, and then dashed full speed across the street. He bounded upwards and his fingers closed on the rough edge of the wall. It was easy for him to pull himself upwards then. The top of the wall was about a foot and a half across and set with a double row of spikes made of iron and about six inches high. Along these was strung a double row of thin wires which glinted in the light from the mansion.

He stepped gingerly over the wires and turned and let himself down over the edge and then dropped to the soft earth. For a few seconds, he looked at the guardhouse and the mansion and listened. He heard nothing and saw no signs of life.

He ran into the bush and picked up the beamer. Getting back over the wall was a little more difficult with the beamer strapped over his shoulder, but he made it without, as far as he knew, attracting any attention from inside the walls.

With the beamer and the Horn, he walked down towards Sunset again. He waited on a corner for about ten minutes before an empty cab came by. When he entered the taxi, he held the case with the beamer against it so that the driver would not see it. Its barrel was too thick to be mistaken for even a shotgun, but the stock made it look too much like a firearm of some sort.

Red Orc's address was in a wealthy district of Pacific Palisades. The house was, like Urthona's, surrounded by a high brick wall. However, the iron gate to the driveway was open. Kickaha slipped through it and towards the house, which was dark. Urthona had not mentioned whether or not he had left guards there, but it seemed reasonable that he would. He would not want to miss a chance to catch Red Orc if he should return for some reason.

The front and rear main entrances were locked. No light shone anywhere. He crouched by each door, his ear against the wood. He could hear nothing. Finally, he bored a hole through the lock of the rear door and pushed it open. His entry was cautious and slow at first and then he heard some noises from the front. These turned out to have been made by three men sitting in the dark in the huge room at the front of the house. One had fallen asleep and was snoring softly, and the other two were talking in low voices.

He sneaked up the winding staircase, which had marble steps and so did not squeak or groan under his feet. Finding a bedroom, he closed the door and then turned on a lamp. He dialled one of the numbers of the house.

When the phone was answered, Kickaha, an excellent mimic, spoke in an approximation of Ramos' voice.

'The boss is calling you guys in,' he said. 'Get out here on the double! Something's up, but I can't tell you over the phone!'

He waited until the man had hung up before he himself hung up. Then he went to the window. He saw the three walk down the driveway and go through the gate. A moment later, the headlights of a car came on a half block down. The car pulled away, and he was, as far as he knew, alone in the house. He would not be for more than thirty-five minutes, at least, which was the time it would take the thugs to get to Urthona's, find out they had been tricked, and return with reinforcements.

All he needed was a few minutes. He went downstairs and turned on the lights in the kitchen. Finding a flashlight, he turned the kitchen lights off and went into the big front room. The door under the stairs was open. He stepped through it into the little hall. At its end, he opened the door and cast the flashlight beam inside. The room looked just like the one he had entered when he was Red Orc's prisoner, but it was not. This room really was set inside this house. The gate embedded in the wood and plaster of the doorway had been inactivated.

He opened the instrument case and took the Horn out. In the beams of the flashlight, it glistened silvery. It was shaped like the horn of an African buffalo except at the mouth, where it flared broadly. The tip was fitted with a mouthpiece of soft golden material, and on top along the axis were seven small buttons in a row. Inside the flared mouth was a silvery web of some material. Halfway along the length of the Horn was an inscribed hieroglyph, the mark of Shambarimen, maker of the Horn.

He raised the Horn to his lips and blew softly through it while he pressed the little buttons. The flare on the other end was pointed at the walls, and, as he finished one sequence of notes, he moved it to his left until it pointed at a place on the wall about twelve feet from the first. He hoped that the inactive gates were in this room. If they were, they had set up a resonant point which had weakened the walls between the universes. And so the frequencies from the Horn would act as a skeleton key and open the gates. This was the unique ability of the Horn, the unreproduced device of Shambarimen, greatest of the scientist-inventors of the Lords.

Softly the Horn spoke, and the notes that issued from the mouth seemed golden and magical enough to open doors to fairyland. But none appeared on the north or east walls. Kickaha stopped blowing and listened for sounds of people approaching the house. He heard nothing. He put the mouthpiece to his lips again and once more played the sequence of notes which was guaranteed to spread wide any break in the walls between the worlds.

Suddenly, a spot on the wall became luminous. The white spot enlarged, inched outwards, and then sprang to the limits of the circle which defined the entrance. The light faded and was replaced by a softer darker light. He looked into it and saw a hemispherical room with no windows or doors. The walls were scarlet, and the only furniture was a bed which floated a few feet above the floor in the centre of the room and a transparent booth, also floating, which contained a washbowl, faucet, and toilet.

Then the walls regrew swiftly, the edges of the hole sliding out towards each other, and, in thirty seconds, the wall was as solid as before.

The Horn swung away, and the white spot appeared again and grew and then the light died to be replaced by the greenish light of a green sun over a green-moss-tinted plain and sharp green mountains on a horizon twice as distant as Earth's. To the right were some animals that looked like gazelles with harp-shaped horns. They were nibbling on the moss.

The third opening revealed a hallway with a closed door at its end. There was nothing else for Kickaha to do but to investigate, since the door might lead to Anana or the others. He jumped through the now swiftly decreasing hole and walked down the hall and then cautiously opened the door. Nothing happened. He looked around the edge of the door into a large chamber. Its floor was stone mosaic, a small pool flush with the floor was in the centre, and furniture of airy construction was around it. The light was sourceless.

Anana, unaware that anybody had entered, was sitting on a chair and reading from a big book with thick covers that looked like veined marble. She looked sleek and well fed.

Kickaha watched her for a minute, though he had to restrain himself from running in and grabbing her. He had lived too long in worlds where traps were baited.

His inspection did not reveal anything suspicious, but this meant only that dangers could be well hidden. Finally, he called softly, 'Anana!'

She jumped, the book fell out of her hands, and then she was out of the chair and rushing towards him. Tears glimmered in her eyes and on her cheeks though she was smiling. Her arms were held out to him, and she was sobbing with relief and joy.

His desire to run towards her was almost overwhelming. He felt tears in his own eyes and a sob welling up. But he could not get rid of his suspiciousness that Red Orc might have set this room to kill a person who entered without first activating some concealed device. He had been lucky to get this far without tripping off some machine.

'Kickaha!' Anana cried and came through the door and fell into his embrace.

He looked over her shoulder to make sure that the door was swinging shut and then bent his head to kiss her.

The pain on his lips and nose was like that from burning gasoline. The pain on the palms of his hand, where he had pressed it against her back, was like that from sulphuric acid.

He screamed and threw himself away and rolled on the floor in his agony. Yet, half-conscious though he was from the searing, he knew that his tortured hand had grabbed the beamer from the floor, where he had dropped it.

Anana came after him but not swiftly. Her face had melted as if it were wax in the sun; her eyes ran; her mouth drooped and furrowed and made runnels and ridges. Her hands were spread out to seize him, but they were dripping with acid and losing form. The fingers had become elongated, so much so that one had stretched down, like taffy, to her knee. And her beautiful legs were bulging everywhere, giving way to something like gas pressing the skin outwards. The feet were splaying out and leaving impresses of something that burned the stone of the floor and gave off faint green wisps of smoke.

The horror of this helped him overcome the pain. Without hesitation, he lifted the beamer and pressed the button that turned its power full on her. Rather, on *it*.

She fell into two and then into four parts as the beam crisscrossed. The parts writhed on the floor, silently. Blood squirted out from the trunks and from the legs and turned into a brownish substance which scorched the stone. An odour as of rotten eggs and burning dog excrement filled the room.

Kickaha stepped down the power from piercing to burning. He played the beam like a hose squirting flaming kerosene over the parts, and they went up in smoke. The hair of Anana burned with all the characteristic odour of burning human hair, but that was the only part of her – of it – that gave off a stench of human flesh in the fire. The rest was brimstone and dog droppings.

In the end, after the fire burned out, there were only some gristly threads left. Of bones there was no sign.

Kickaha did not wish to enter the room from which it had come, but the pain in his lips and nose and hand was too intense. Besides, he thought that the Lord should have been satisfied with the fatality of the thing he had created to look like Anana. There was cool-looking water in that room, and he had to have it. It was possible to blow the Horn and go back into Orc's office, but he did not think he could endure the agony long enough to blow the sequence of notes. Moreover, if he encountered anyone in that office, he wanted to be able to defend himself adequately. In his present condition, he could not.

At the pool he stuck his face and one hand under the water. The coolness seemed to help at once, although when he at last removed his face and breathed, the pain was still intense. With the good hand, he splashed water on his face. After a long while, he rose from the pool. He was unsteady and felt as if he were going to vomit. He also felt a little disengaged from everything. The shock had nudged him one over from reality.

When he raised the Horn gently to his lips, he found that they were swelling. His hand was also swelling. They were getting so big and stiff they were making him clumsy. It was only at the cost of more agony that he could blow upon the Horn and press the little valves, and the wall opened before him. He quickly put the Horn in its case, and shoved it through the opening with his foot, then leaped through with the beamer ready. The office was empty.

He found the bathroom. The medicine cabinet above the washbowl was a broad and deep one with many bottles. A number were of plastic, marked with hieroglyphs. He opened one, smelled the contents, tried to grin with his blistered swollen lips and squeezed out a greenish salve onto his hand. This he rubbed over his nose and lips and on the palm of his burned hand. Immediately, the pain began to dissolve in a soft coolness and the swelling subsided as he watched himself in the mirror.

He squeezed a few drops from another bottle onto his tongue, and a minute later the shakiness and the sense of unreality left him. He recapped the two bottles and put them in the rear pockets of his pants.

The business of the gates and the Anana-thing had taken more time than he could spare. He ran out of the bathroom and directed the Horn at the next spot on the wall. This failed to respond, so he tried the next one. This one opened, but neither this nor the one after it contained those for whom he was looking.

The bedroom yielded a gate at the first place he directed the Horn. The wall parted like an opening mouth, a shark's mouth, because the hillside beyond was set with rows of tall white sharp triangles. The vegetation between the shark's teeth was a purplish vine-complex and the sky beyond was mauve.

The second gate opened to another hallway with a door at its end. Again, he had no choice except to investigate. He pushed the door open silently and peered around it. The room looked exactly like the one in which he had found the thing he had thought was Anana. This time, she was not reading a book, although she was in the chair. She was leaning far forward, her elbows on her thighs and her chin cupped by her hands. Her stare was unmoving and gloomy.

He called to her softly, and she jumped, just like the first Anana. Then she leaped up and ran towards him, tears in her eyes and on her cheeks and her mouth open in a beautiful smile and her arms held towards him. He backed away as she came through the door and harshly told her to stop. He held the beamer on her. She obeyed but looked puzzled and hurt. Then she saw the still slightly swelled and burned lips and nose, and her eyes widened.

'Anana,' he said, 'what was that ten-thousand-year-old nursery rhyme your mother sang to you so often?'

If this was some facsimile or artificial creature of Red Orc's, it might have a recording of some of what Orc had learned from Anana. It might have a memory of a sort, something that would be sketchy but still adequate enough to fool her lover. But there would be things she had not told Red Orc while under the influence of the drug because he would not think to ask her. And the nursery song was one thing. She had told Kickaha of it when they had been hiding from the Bellers on the Great Plain of the World of Tiers.

Anana was more puzzled for a few seconds, and then she seemed to understand that he felt compelled to test her. She smiled and sang the beautiful little song that her mother had taught her in the days before she grew up and found out how ugly and vicious the adult family life of the Lords was.

Even after this, he felt restrained when he kissed her. Then, as it became apparent that she had to be genuine flesh and blood, and she murmured a few more things that Red Orc was highly unlikely to know, he smiled and melted. They both cried some more, but he stopped first.

'We'll weep a little later,' he said. 'Do you have any idea where Wolff and Chryseis could be?'

She said no, which was what he had expected.

'Then we'll use the Horn until we've opened every gate in the house. But it's a big house, so . . .'

He explained to her that Urthona and his men would be coming after them. 'You look around for weapons, while I blow the Horn.'

She joined him ten minutes later and showed him what looked like a pen but was a small beamer. He told her that he had found two more gates but both were disappointments. They passed swiftly through all the rooms in the second storey while he played steadily upon the Horn. The walls remained blank.

The first floor of the house was as unrewarding. By then, forty minutes had passed since the men had left the house. Within a few more minutes, Urthona should be here.

'Let's try the room under the stairs again,' he said. 'It's possible that reactivating the gate might cause it to open onto still another world.'

A gate could be set up so that it alternated its resonances slightly and acted as a flipflop entrance. At one activation, it would open to one universe and at the next activation, to another. Some gates could operate as avenues to a dozen or more worlds.

The gates activated upstairs could also be such gates, and they should return to test out the multiple activity of every one. It was too discouraging to think about at that moment, though they would have to run through them again. That is, they would if this gate under the stairs did not give them a pleasant surprise.

Outside the door, he lifted the Horn once more and played the music which trembled the fabric between universes. The room beyond the door suddenly was large and blue-walled with bright lights streaming from chandeliers carved out of single Brobdingnagian jewels: hippopotamus-head-sized diamonds, rubies, emeralds, and garnets. The furniture was also carved out of enormous jewels set together with some kind of golden cement.

Kickaha had seen even more luxurious rooms. What held his attention was the opening of the round door at the far end of the room and the entrance through it of a cylindrical object. This was dark red, and it floated a foot above the floor. At its distant end the top of a blond head appeared. A man was pushing the object towards them.

That head looked like Red Orc's. He seemed to be the only one who would be in another world and bringing towards this gate an object that undoubtedly meant death and destruction to the occupants of this house.

Kickaha had his beamer ready, but he did not fire it. If that cylinder was packed with some powerful explosive, it might go up at the touch of the energy in the ray from a beamer.

Quickly, but silently, he began to close the door. Anana looked puzzled, since she had not seen what he had. He whispered, 'Take off out the front door and run as far as you can as fast as you can!'

She shook her head and said, 'Why should I?'

'Here!'

He thrust the Horn and the case at her. 'Beat it! Don't argue! If he . . .'

The door began to swing open. A thin curved instrument came around the side of the door. Kickaha fired at it, cutting it in half. There was a yell from the other side, cut off by the door slamming. Kickaha had shoved it hard with his foot.

'Run!' he yelled, and he took her hand and pulled her

after him. Just as he went through the door, he looked back. There was a crash as the door under the stairs and part of the wall around it fell broken outwards, and the cylinder thrust halfway through before stopping.

That was enough for Kickaha. He jumped out onto the porch and down the steps, pulling Anana behind him with one hand, the other holding the beamer. When they reached the brick wall by the sidewalk, he turned to run along it for its protection.

The expected explosion did not come immediately.

At that moment, a car screeched around the corner a block away. It straightened up, swaying under the street lights, and shot towards the driveway of the house they had just left. Kickaha saw the silhouettes of six heads inside it; one might have been Urthona's. Then he was running again. They rounded the corner from which the speeding automobile had come, and still nothing happened. Anana cried out, but he continued to drag her on. They ran a complete block and were crossing the street to go around another corner, when a black and white patrol car came by. It was cruising slowly and so the occupants had plenty of time to see the two runners. Anybody walking on the streets after dark in this area was suspect. A running person was certain to be taken to the station for questioning. Two running persons carrying a large musical instrument case and something that looked like a peculiar shotgun were guaranteed capture by the police. If they could be caught, of course.

Kickaha cursed and darted towards the house nearest them. Its lights were on, and the front door was open, though the screen door was probably locked. Behind them, brakes squealed as the patrol car slid to a stop. A loud voice told them to stop.

They continued to run. They ran onto the porch and Kickaha pulled on the screen door. He intended to go right through the house and out the back door, figuring that the police were not likely to shoot at them if innocents were in the way.

Kickaha cursed, gave the handle of the screen door a

yank that tore the lock out. He plunged through with Anana right behind him. They shot through a vestibule and into a large room with a chandelier and a broad winding staircase to the second storey. There were about ten men and women standing or sitting, all dressed semiformally. The women screamed; the men yelled. The two intruders ran through them, unhindered while the shouts of the policemen rose above the noise of the occupants.

The next moment, all human noise was shattered. The blast smashed in the glass of the windows and shook the house as if a tidal wave had struck it. All were hurled to the floor by the impact.

Kickaha had been expecting this, and Anana had expected something enormously powerful by his behaviour. They jumped up before anybody else could regain their wits and were going out the back door in a few seconds. Kickaha doubled back, running towards the front along the side of the house. There was much broken glass on the walk, flicked there by the explosion from some nearby house. A few bushes and some lawn furniture also lay twisted on the sidewalk.

The patrol car, its motor running, and lights on, was still by the kerb. Anana threw the instrument case into the rear seat and got in and Kickaha laid the beamer on the floor and climbed in. They strapped themselves in, and he turned the car around and took off. In the course of the next four blocks, he found the button switches to set the siren off and the light whirling and flashing.

'We'll get to Urthona's house, near it, anyway,' he yelled, 'and then we'll abandon this. I think Red Orc'll be there now to find out if Urthona was among those who entered the house when that mine went off!'

Anana shook her head and pointed at her ears. She was still deaf.

It was no wonder. He could just faintly hear the siren which must be screaming in their ears.

A few minutes later, as they shot through a red light, they passed a patrol car, lights flashing, going the other way. Anana ducked down so that she would not be seen, but evidently the car had received notice by radio that this car was stolen. It screamed as it slowed down and turned on the broad intersection and started after Kickaha and Anana. A sports car which had sped through the intersections, as if its driver intended to ignore the flashing red lights and sirens, turned away to avoid a collision, did not quite make it, scraped against the rear of the police car, and caromed off over the kerbing, and up onto the sidewalk.

Kickaha saw this in the mirror as he accelerated. A few minutes later, he went through a stop sign south of a very broad intersection with stop signs on all corners. A big Cadillac stopped in the middle of the intersection so suddenly that its driver went up over the wheel. Before he could sit back and continue, the patrol car came through the stop sign.

Kickaha said, 'Can you hear me now?'

She said, 'Yes. You don't have to shout quite so loudly!'

'We're in Beverly Hills now. We'll take this car as far as we can and then we'll abandon it, on the run,' he said. 'We'll have to lose them on foot. That is, if we make it.'

A second patrol car had joined them. It had come out of a side street, ignoring a stop sign, causing another car to wheel away and ram into the kerbing. Its driver had hoped to cut across in front of them and bar their way, but he had not been quite fast enough. Kickaha had the car up to eighty now, which was far too fast on this street with its many intersecting side streets.

Then the business section of Beverly Hills was ahead. The light changed to yellow just as Kickaha zoomed through. He blasted the horn and went around a sports car and skidded a little and then the car hit a dip and bounced into the air. He had, however, put on the brakes to slow to sixty. Even so, the car swayed so that he feared they were going over.

Ahead of them, a patrol car was approaching. It swung broadside when over a half block away and barred most of the street. There was very little clearance at either end of the patrol car, but Kickaha took the rear.

Both uniformed policemen were out of the car, one behind the hood with a shotgun and the other standing between the front of the car and the parked cars. Kickaha told Anana to duck and took the car between the narrow space on the other side. There was a crash, the car struck the side of the bumper of the patrol car and the other struck the side of a parked car. But they were through with a grinding and clashing of metal. The shotgun boomed; the rear window starred.

At the same time, another patrol car swung around the corner on their left. The car angled across the street. Kickaha slammed on the brakes. They screamed, and he was pushed forward against his belt and the wheel. The car fishtailed, rocked, and then it slammed at an obtuse angle into the front of the patrol car.

Both cars were out of commission. Kickaha and Anana were stunned, but they reacted on pure reflex. They were out of the car on either side, Kickaha holding the beamer, and Anana the instrument case. They ran across the street, between two parked cars, and across the sidewalk before they heard the shouts of the policemen behind them. Then they were between two tall buildings on a narrow sidewalk bordered by trees and bushes. They dashed down this until they came out on the next street. Here Kickaha led her northward, saw another opening between buildings, and took that. There was an overhang of prestressed concrete about eight feet up over a doorway. He threw his beamer upon it, threw the instrument case up, turned, held his locked hands out, and she put her foot in it and went up as he heaved. She caught the edge of the overhang: he pushed, and she was up on it. He leaped and swung on up, lying down just in time.

Feet pounded; several men, breathing hard, passed under them. He risked a peep over the edge and saw three policemen at the far end of the passageway, outlined by the streetlights. They were talking, obviously puzzled by the disappearance of their quarry. Then one started back, and Kickaha flattened out. The other two went around the corner of the building.

But as the man passed below him, Kickaha, taken by a

sudden idea, rose and leaped upon the man. He knocked him sprawling, hitting the man so hard he knocked the wind out of him. He followed this with a kick on the jaw.

Kickaha put the officer's cap on and emptied the .38 which he took from his holster. Anana swung down after having dropped the beamer and the Horn to him. She said, 'Why did you do this?'

'He would have blocked our retreat. Besides, there's a car that isn't damaged, and we're going to take that.'

The fourth policeman was sitting in the car and talking over a microphone. He did not see Kickaha until he was about forty paces away. He dropped the microphone and grabbed for the shotgun on the seat. The beamer, set for stunning power, hit him in the shoulder and knocked him against the car. He slumped down, the shotgun falling on the street.

Kickaha pulled the officer away from the car, noting that blood was seeping through his shirt sleeve. The beamer, even when set on 'stun' power, could smash bone, tear skin, and rupture blood vessels.

As soon as Anana was in the car, Kickaha turned it northwards. Down the street, coming swiftly towards him, on the wrong side because the other lane was blocked, were two police cars.

At the intersection ahead, as Kickaha shot past the red light, he checked his rear view mirror and saw the police cars had turned and were speeding after him.

Ahead the traffic was so heavy, he had no chance of getting onto it or across it. There was nothing to do but to take the alley to the right or the left, and he took the left. This was by the two-storey brick wall of a grocery store building.

Then he was down the alley. Kickaha applied his brakes so hard, the car swerved, scraping against the brick wall. Anana scrambled out after Kickaha on his side of the car.

The police cars, moving more slowly than Kickaha's had when it took the corner into the alley, turned in. Just as the first straightened out to enter, Kickaha shot at the tyres.

The front of the lead car dropped as if it had driven off a kerb, and there was a squeal of brakes.

The car rocked up and down, and then its front doors opened like the wings of a bird just before taking off.

Kickaha ran away with Anana close behind him. He led her at an angle across the parking lot of the grocery store, and through the driveway out onto the street.

The light was red now, and the cars were stopped. Kickaha ran up behind a sports car in which sat a small youth with long black hair, huge round spectacles, a hawkish nose, and a bristly black moustache. He was tapping on the instrument panel with his right hand to the raucous cacophonous radio music, which was like Scylla and Charybdis rubbing against each other. He stiffened when Kickaha's arm shot down, as unexpectedly as a lightning stroke from a clear sky, over his shoulder and onto his lap. Before he could do more than squeak and turn his head, the safety belt was unbuckled. Like a sack of flour, he came out of the seat at the end of Kickaha's arm and was hurled onto the sidewalk. The dispossessed driver lay stunned for a moment and then leaped screaming with fury to his feet. By then, Kickaha and Anana were in his car, on their way.

Anana, looking behind, said, 'We got away just in time.'

'Any police cars after us?' he said.

'No. Not yet.'

'Good. We only have a couple of miles to go.'

There was no sign of the police from there on until Kickaha parked the car a block and a half from Urthona's.

He said, 'I've described the layout of the house, so you won't get confused when we're in it. Once we get in, things may go fast and furious. I think Red Orc will be there. I believe he's gated there just to make sure that Urthona is dead. He may be alive, though, because he's a fox. He should have scented a trap. I know I would've been skittish about going into that house unless I'd sniffed around a lot.'

The house was well lit, but there was no sign of occupants. They walked boldly up the front walk and onto the porch. Kickaha tried the door and found it locked. A quick circling of the beamer muzzle with piercing power turned on removed the lock mechanism. They entered a silent house and when they were through exploring it, they had found only a parrot in a cage and it broke the silence only once to give a muffled squawk.

Kickaha removed the Horn from the case and began to test for resonant points as he had at Red Orc's. He went from room to room, working out from Urthona's bedroom and office because the gates were most likely to be there. The Horn sent out its melodious notes in vain, however, until he stuck it into a large closet downstairs just off the bottom of the staircase. The wall issued a tiny white spot, like a tear of light, and then it expanded and suddenly became a hole into another world.

Kickaha got a glimpse of a room that was a duplicate of the closet in the house in which he stood. Anana cried out softly then and pulled at his arm. He turned, hearing the noise that had caused her alarm. There were footsteps on the porch, followed by the chiming of the doorbell. He strode across the room, stopped halfway, turned and tossed the Horn to her, and said, 'Keep that gate open!' While the notes of the Horn travelled lightly across the room, he lifted the curtain a little. Three uniformed policemen were on the porch and a plainclothesman was just going around the side. On the street were two patrol cars and an unmarked automobile.

Kickaha returned to her and said, 'Urthona must have had a man outside watching for us. He called the cops. They must have the place surrounded!'

They could try to fight their way out, surrender, or go through the gate. To do the first was to kill men whose only fault was to mistake Kickaha as a criminal.

If Kickaha surrendered, he would sentence himself and Anana to death. Once either of the Lords knew they were in prison, they would get to their helpless victims one way or the other and murder them.

He did not want to go through the gate without taking some precautions, but he had no choice. He said, 'Let's go,' and leaped through the contracting hole with his beamer ready. Anana, holding onto the Horn, followed him.

He kicked the door open and jumped back. After a minute of waiting, he stepped through it. The closet was set near the bottom of a staircase, just like its counterpart on Earth. The room was huge with marble walls on which were bright murals and a many-coloured marble mosaic floor. It was night outside, the light inside came from many oil-burning lamps and cressets on the walls and the fluted marble pillars around the edges of the room. Beyond, in the shadows cast by the pillars, were entrances to other rooms and to the outside.

There was no sound except for a hissing and sputtering from the flames at the ends of the cressets.

Kickaha walked across the room between the pillars and through an antechamber, the walls of which were decorated with dolphins and octopuses. It was these that made him expect the scene that met him when he stepped out upon the great pillared porch. He was back on Earth Number Two.

At least, it seemed that he was. Certainly, the full moon near the zenith was Earth's moon. And, looking down from the porch, which was near the edge of a small mountain, he would swear that he was looking down on the duplicate of that part of southern California on which Los Angeles of Earth Number One was built. As nearly as he could tell in the darkness, it had the same topography. The unfamiliarity was caused by the differences in the two cities. This one was smaller than Los Angeles; the lights were not so many nor so bright, and were more widely spaced. He would guess that the population of this valley was about one thirty-second of Earth Number One.

The air looked clear; the stars and the moon were large and bright. There was no hint of the odour of gasoline. He could smell a little horse manure, but that was pleasant, very pleasant.

Of course, he was basing his beliefs on very small evidence, but it seemed that the technology of this Earth had not advanced nearly as swiftly as that of his native planet.

Evidently, Urthona had found gates leading to this world.

He heard voices then from the big room into which he had emerged from the closet. He took Anana's arm and pulled her with him into the shadow of a pillar. Immediately thereafter, three people stepped out onto the porch. Two were men, wearing kilts and sandals and cloth jackets with flared-out collars, puffed sleeves, and swallow tails. One was short, dark and Mediterranean, like the servants of Red Orc. The other was tall, ruddy-faced and reddish-haired. The woman was a short blonde with a chunky figure. She wore a kilt, buskins and a jacket also, but the jacket, unbuttoned, revealed bare breasts held up by a stiff shelf projecting from a flaming red corselet. Her hair was piled high in an ornate coiffure, and her face was heavily made up. She shivered, said something in a Semitic-sounding language, and buttoned up the jacket.

If these were servants, they were able to ride in style. A carriage like a cabriolet, drawn by two handsome horses, came around the corner and stopped before the porch. The coachman jumped down and assisted them into the carriage. He wore a tall tricorn hat with a bright red feather, a jacket with huge gold buttons and scarlet piping, a heavy blue kilt, and calf-length boots.

The three got into the carriage and drove off. Kickaha watched the oil-burning lamps on the cabriolet until they were out of sight on the road that wound down the mountain.

This world, Kickaha thought, would be fascinating to investigate. Physically, it had been exactly like the other Earth when it had started. And its peoples, created fifteen thousand years ago, had been exactly like those of the other Earth. Twins, they had been placed in the same locations, given the same languages and the same rearing, and then were left to themselves. He supposed that the deviations of the humans here from those on his world had started almost immediately. Fifteen millennia had resulted in very different histories and cultures.

He would like to stay here and wander over the face of this Earth. But now, he had to find Wolff and Chryseis and to do this he would have to find and capture Urthona.

The only action available was to use the Horn, and to hope it would reveal the right gate to the Lord.

This was not going to be easy, as he found out a few minutes later. The Horn, though not loud, attracted several servants. Kickaha fired the beamer once at a pillar near them. They saw the hole appear in the stone and, shouting and screaming, fled. Kickaha urged Anana to continue blowing the Horn, but the uproar from the interior convinced him that they could not remain here. This building was too huge for them to leisurely investigate the first storey. The most likely places for gates were in the bedroom or office of the master, and these were probably on the second storey.

When they were halfway up the steps, a number of men with steel conical helmets, small round shields, and swords and spears appeared. There were, however, three men who carried big heavy clumsy-looking firearms with flared muzzles, wooden stocks, and flintlocks.

Kickaha cut the end of one blunderbuss off with the beamer. The men scattered, but they regrouped before Kickaha and Anana had reached the top of the steps. Kickaha cut through the bottom of a marble pillar and then through the top. The pillar fell over with a crash that shook the house, and the armed men fled.

It was a costly rout, because a little knob on the side of the beamer suddenly flashed a red light. There was not much charge left, and he did not have another powerpack.

They found a bedroom that seemed to be that of the Lord's. It was certainly magnificent enough, but everything in this mansion was magnificent. It contained a number of weapons, swords, axes, daggers, throwing knives, maces, rapiers, and – delight! – bows and a quiver of arrows. While Anana probed the walls and floors with the Horn, Kickaha chose a knife with a good balance for her and then strung a bow. He shouldered a quiver and felt much better. The beamer had enough left in it for several seconds of full piercing power or a dozen or so rays of burn power or several score rays of stun power. After that, he would have to depend on his primitive weapons.

He also chose a light axe that seemed suitable for throwing for Anana. She was proficient in the use of all weapons and, while she was not as strong as he, she was as skilful.

She stopped blowing the Horn. There was a bed which hung by golden chains from the ceiling, and beyond it on the wall was a spreading circle of light. The light dissolved to show delicate pillars supporting a frescoed ceiling and, beyond, many trees.

Anana cried out with surprise in which was an anguished delight. She started forward but was held back by Kickaha. He said, 'What's the hurry?'

'It's home!' she said. 'Home!'

Her whole being seemed to radiate light.

'Your world?' he said.

'Oh, no! Home! Where I was born! The world where the Lords originated!'

There did not seem to be any traps, but that meant nothing. However, the hubbub outside the room indicated that they had better move on or expect to fight. Since the beamer was so depleted, he could not fight them off for long, not if they were persistent.

He said, 'Here we go' and leaped through. Anana had to bend low and scoot through swiftly, because the circle was closing. When she got up on her feet, she said, 'Do you remember that tall building on Wilshire, near the tar pits? The big one with the big sign, *California Federal*? It was always ablaze with lights at night?'

He nodded and she said, 'This summerhouse is exactly on that spot. I mean, on the place that corresponds to that spot.'

There was no sign of anything corresponding to Wilshire Boulevard, nothing resembling a road or even a foot path here. The number of trees here certainly did take away from the southern California lowlands look, but she explained that the Lords had created rivers and brooks here so that this forest could grow. The summerhouse was one of many built so that the family could stop for the night or retire for meditation or the doing of whatever virtue or vice they felt like. The main dwellings were all on the beach.

There had never been many people in this valley, and, when Anana was born, only three families lived here. Later, at least as far as she knew, all the Lords had left this valley. In fact, they had left this world to occupy their own artificial universes and from thence to wage their wars upon each other.

Kickaha allowed her to wander around while she exclaimed softly to herself or called to him to look at something that she suddenly remembered. He wondered that she remembered anything at all, since her last visit here had been three thousand and two hundred years ago. When he thought of this, he asked her where the gate was through which she had entered at that time.

'It's on top of a boulder about a half mile from here,' she said. 'There are a number of gates, all disguised, of course. And nobody knows how many others here. I didn't know about the one under the stone floor of the summerhouse, of course. Urthona must have put it there long ago, maybe ten thousand years ago.'

'This summerhouse is that old?'

'That old. It contains self-renewing and self-cleaning equipment, of course. And equipment to keep the forest and the land in its primeval state is under the surface. Erosion and buildup of land are compensated for.'

'Are there any weapons hidden here for your use?' he said.

'There are a number just within the gate,' she said. 'But the charges will have trickled off to nothing by now, and, besides, I don't have an activator....'

She stopped and said, 'I forgot about the Horn. It can activate the gate, of course, but there's really nothing in it to help us.'

'Where does the gate lead to?'

'It leads to a room which contains another gate, and this one opens directly to the interior of the palace of my own world. But it is trapped. I had to leave my deactivator behind when the Bellers invaded my world and I escaped through another gate into Jadawin's world.'

'Show me where the boulder is, anyway. If we have to, we could take refuge inside its gate and come back out later.'

First, they must eat and, if possible, take a nap. Anana took him into the house, although she first studied it for a long time for traps. The kitchen contained an exquisitely sculptured marble cabinet. This, in turn, housed a fabricator, the larger part of which was buried under the house. Anana opened it cautiously and set the controls, closed it, and a few minutes later opened it again. There were two trays with dishes and cups of delicious food and drink. The energy-matter converters below the earth had been waiting for thousands of years to serve this meal and would wait another hundred thousand years to serve the next one if events so proceeded.

After eating, they stretched out on a bed which hung on chains from the ceiling. Kickaha questioned her about the layout of the land. She was about to go to sleep when he said, 'I've had the feeling that we got here not entirely by accident. I think either Urthona or Red Orc set it up so that we'd get here if we were fast and clever enough. And he also set it up so that the other Lord, his enemy, would be here, if the other Lord is alive. I feel that this is the showdown, and that Urthona or Orc arranged to have it here for poetic or aesthetic reasons. It would be like a Lord to bring his enemies back to the home planet to kill them – if he could. This is just a feeling, but I'm going to act as if it were definite knowledge.'

'You'd act that way, anyway,' she said. 'But I think you may be right.'

She fell asleep. He left the bed and went to the front room to watch. The sun started down from the zenith. Beautiful birds, most of whose ancestors must have been made in the biolabs of the Lords, gathered around the fountain and pool before the house. Once, a large brown bear ambled through the trees and near the house. Another time, he heard a sound that tingled his nerves and filled him with joy. It was the shrill trumpet of a mammoth. Its cry reminded him of the Amerind tier of Wolff's world, where mammoths and mastodons by the millions roamed the plains and the forests of an area larger than all of North and South America. He felt homesick and wondered when – if – he would ever see that world again. The Hrowakas, the Bear People, the beautiful and the great Amerinds who had adopted him, were dead now, murdered by the Bellers. But there were other tribes who would be eager to adopt him, even those who called him their greatest enemy and had been trying for years to lift his scalp or his head.

He returned to the bedroom and awoke Anana, telling her to rouse him in about an hour. She did so, and though he would have liked to sleep for the rest of the day and half the night, he forced himself to get up.

They ate some more food and packed more in a small basket. They set off through the woods, which were thick with trees but only moderately grown with underbrush. They came onto a trail which had been trampled by mammoths, as the tracks and droppings showed. They followed this, sensitive for the trumpetings or squealings of the big beasts. There were no flies or mosquitoes, but there was a variety of large beetles and other insects on which the birds fed.

Once, they heard a savage yowl. They stopped, then continued after it was not repeated. Both recognized the cry of the sabertooth.

'If this was the estate of your family, why did they keep the big dangerous beasts around?' he said.

'You should know that. The Lords like danger; it is the only spice of eternity. Immortality is nothing unless it can be taken away from you at any moment.'

That was true. Only those who had immortality could appreciate that. But he wished, sometimes, that there were not so much spice. Lately, he did not seem to be getting enough rest, and his nerves were raw from the chafing of continuous peril.

'Do you think that anybody else would know about the gate in the boulder?'

'Nothing is sure,' she replied. 'But I do not think so. Why? Do you think that Urthona will know that we'll be going to the boulder?'

'It seems highly probable. Otherwise, he would have set up a trap for us at the summerhouse. I think that he may expect and want us to go to the boulder because he is also leading another towards the same place. It's to be a trysting place for us and our two enemies.'

'You don't know that. It's just your highly suspicious mind believing that things are as you would arrange them if you were a Lord.'

'Look who's calling who paranoid,' he said, smiling. 'Maybe you're right. But I've been through so much that I can hear the tumblers of other people's minds clicking.'

He decided that Anana should handle the beamer and he would have his bow and arrows ready.

Near the edge of the clearing, Kickaha noted a slight swelling in the earth. It was almost a quarter inch high and two inches wide, and it ran for several feet, then disappeared. He moved in a zigzagging path for several yards and finally found another swelling which described a small part of a very large circle before it disappeared, too.

He went back to Anana, who had been watching him with a puzzled expression.

'Do you know of any underground work done around here?' he said.

'No,' she said. 'Why?'

'Maybe an earthquake did it,' he said and did not comment any more on the swelling.

The boulder was about the size of a one-bedroom bungalow and was set near the edge of a clearing. It was of red and black granite and had been transported here from the north along with thousands of other boulders to add variety to the landscape. It was about a hundred yards northeast of a tar pit. This pit, Kickaha realized, was the same size and in the same location as the tar pit in Hancock Park on Earth Number One.

They got down on their bellies and snaked slowly towards the boulder. When they were within thirty yards of it, Kickaha crawled around until he was able to see all sides of the huge rock. Coming back, he said, 'I didn't think he'd be dumb enough to hide *behind* it. But *in* it would be a good move. Or maybe he's out in the woods and waiting for us to open the gate because he's trapped it.'

'If you're right and he's waiting for a third party to show . . .'

She stopped and clutched his arm and said, 'I saw someone! There!'

She pointed across the clearing at the thick woods where the Los Angeles County Art Museum would have been if this had been Earth Number one. He looked but could see nothing.

'It was a man, I'm sure of that,' she said. 'A tall man. I think he was Red Orc!'

'See any weapon? A beamer?'

'No. I just got a glimpse, and then he was gone behind a tree.'

Kickaha began to get even more uneasy.

He watched the birds and noticed that a raven was cawing madly near where Anana thought she had seen Red Orc. Suddenly, the bird fell off its branch and was seen and heard no more. Kickaha grinned. The Lord had realized it might be giving him away and had shot it.

A hundred yards to their left near the edge of the tar pit, several bluejays screamed and swooped down again and again at something in the tall grass. Kickaha watched them, but in a minute a red fox trotted out of the grass and headed into the woods southward. The jays followed him.

With their departure, a relative quiet arrived. It was hot in the tall saw-bladed grass. Occasionally, a large insect buzzed nearby. Once, a shadow flashed by them, and Kickaha, looking upwards, saw a dragon fly, shimmering golden-green, transparent copper-veined wings at least two feet from tip to tip, zooming by.

Now and then, a trumpeting floated to them and a wolf-like howl came from far beyond. And, once, a big bird high above screamed harshly.

Neither saw a sign of the man Anana had thought was Red Orc. Yet, he must be out there somewhere. He might even have spotted them and be crawling towards their hiding place. This caused Kickaha to move away from their position near the boulder. They did this very slowly so they would shake the tall grasses as unviolently as possible. When they had gotten under the trees at the edge of the clearing, he said, 'We shouldn't stay together. I'm going to go back into the woods about fifty feet or so. I can get a better view.'

He kissed her cheek and crawled off. After looking around, he decided to take a post behind a bush on a slight rise in the ground. There was a tree behind it which would hide him from anybody approaching in that direction. It also had the disadvantage that it could hide the approaching person from him, but he took the chance. And the small height gave him a better view while the bush hid him from those below.

He could not see Anana even though he knew her exact position. Several times, the grasses moved just a little bit contrary to the direction of the breeze. If Orc or Urthona were watching, they would note this and perhaps . . .

He froze. The grass was bending, very slightly and slowly and at irregular intervals, about twenty yards to the right of Anana. There was no movement for what seemed like ten minutes, and then the grass bent again. It pointed towards Anana and moved back up gently, as if somebody were slowly releasing it. A few minutes later, it moved again.

Kickaha was absorbed in watching the progress of the person in the grass, but he did not allow it to distract him from observation elsewhere. During one of his many glances behind him, he saw a flash of white skin through the branches of a bush about sixty feet to his left. At first, he considered moving away from his position to another. But if he did so, he would very probably be seen by the newcomer. It was possible that he had been seen already. The best action just now was no action.

The sun slid on down the sky, and the shadows lengthened. The person creeping towards Anana moved rarely and very slowly but within an hour he was about twelve feet from her. Whether or not she knew it, Kickaha could not tell.

He removed the Horn from its case. And he placed the nock of an arrow in the string of the bow and waited. Again, the grass bent down towards Anana, and the person moved a foot closer.

Behind him, nothing showed except the flash of a bright blue-and-red bird swooping between two trees.

Presently, on the other side of the clearing, keeping close to the trees on its edge, a huge black wolf trotted. It stood at least four and a half feet high at the shoulder, and it could remove the leg of a man at the ankle bone with one bite. It was a dire wolf, extinct on Earth some ten thousand years, but plentiful on Jadawin's world and recreated in the Lords' biolabs for restocking of this area. The giant he-wolf trotted along as stealthily and vibrantly as a tiger, its red tongue hanging out like a flag after a heavy rain. It trotted warily but confidently along for twenty yards and then froze. For a few seconds, it turned its head to scan a quarter of the compass, and then it moved ahead, but crouchingly. Kickaha watched it, while keeping tabs on the persons unknown before and behind him – or tried to do so. Thus, he almost missed the quick action of the wolf.

It suddenly charged towards a spot inside the woods and just as suddenly abandoned its charge and fled yowling across the clearing towards Anana. The fur on its back and hind legs was aflame.

Kickaha grasped immediately that a fifth person was in the game and that he had tried to scare the wolf away with a brief power-reduced shot from a beamer. But in his haste he had set the power too high and had burned the wolf instead of just stunning him.

Or perhaps the burning was done deliberately. The newcomer might have set the beast on fire and be guiding him this way with stabs of beamer power to see what he could flush up.

Whatever his intent, he had upset the plans of the person sneaking up on Anana. He had also upset Anana, who, hearing the frantic yowls approaching her with great speed, could not resist raising her head just high enough to see what was happening.

Kickaha wanted to take another quick look behind him, but he did not have time. He rose, bent the bow and released the shaft just as something dark reared up a little way above the grass about forty feet from Anana. It was dressed in black and had a black helmet with a dark faceplate, just like the helmets with visors that the Los Angeles motorcyclists wore. The man held the stock of a short-barreled beamer to his shoulder.

At the same time, the wolf ran howling by, the flames leaping off onto the dry grass and the grass catching fire. The arrow streaked across the space between the trees and the edge of the clearing, the sun sparkling off the metal head. It struck the man just under the left arm, which was raised to hold the barrel of the beamer. The arrow bounced off, but the man, although protected by some sort of flexible armour, was knocked over by the impact of the arrow.

The beamer fell out of his hands. Since it had just been turned on, it cut a fiery tunnel through the grass. It also cut off the front legs of the wolf, which fell down howling but became silent as the beam sliced through its body. The fire, originating from the two sources, quickly spread. Smoke poured out, but Kickaha could see that Anana had not been hit and that she was crawling swiftly through the grass towards the fallen man and the beamer.

Kickaha whirled then, drawing another arrow from the quiver and starting to set it to the bowstring. He saw the tall figure of the man lean from around behind the trunk of a tree. A hand beamer was sticking out, pointing towards Kickaha. Kickaha jumped behind his tree and crouched, knowing that he could not get off an arrow swiftly or accurately enough.

There was a burning odour, a thump. He looked up. The beam had cut through the trunk, and the upper part of the tree had dropped straight down for two inches, its smoothly chopped butt against the top of the stump.

Kickaha stepped to the left side of the tree and shot with all the accuracy of thousands of hours of practice under deliberately difficult conditions and scores of hours in combat. The arrow was so close to the tree, it was deflected by the slightest contact. It zoomed off, just missing the arm of the man holding the beamer. The beamer withdrew as the man jumped back. And then the tree above Kickaha fell over, pulled to one side by the unevenness of the branches' weight. It came down on Kickaha, who jumped back and so escaped the main weight of the trunk. But a branch struck him, and everything became as black and unknowing as the inside of a tree.

When he saw light again, he also saw that not much time had passed. The sun had not moved far. His head hurt as if a root had grown into it and was entangled with the most sensitive nerves. A branch pressed down his chest, and his legs felt as if another branch was weighting them down. He could move his arms a little to one side and turn his head, but otherwise he was as unable to move as if he were buried under a landslide.

Smoke drifted by and made him cough. Flames crackled, and he could feel some heat on the bottom of his feet. The realization that he might burn to death sent him into a frenzy of motion. The result was that his head hurt even more and he had not been able to get out from under the branches at all.

He thought of the others. What had happened to Anana? Why wasn't she here trying to get him free? And the man who had severed the tree? Was he sneaking up now, not sure that he had hit the archer? And then there was the man in black he'd knocked down with the arrow and the person across the clearing who had set fire to the wolf and precipitated the action. Where were they?

If Anana did not do something quickly, she might as well forget about him. The smoke was getting thicker, and his feet and the lower part of his legs were getting very uncomfortable. It would be a question of whether he choked to death from smoke or burned first. Could this be the end? The end came to everybody, even those Lords who had survived fifteen thousand years. But if he had to die, let him do it in his beloved adopted world, the World of Tiers.

Then he stopped thinking such thoughts. He was not dead and he was not going to quit struggling. Somehow, he would get this tree off his chest and legs and would crawl away to where the fire could not reach him and where he would be hidden from his enemies. But where was Anana?

A voice made him start. It came a foot away from his left ear. He turned his head and saw the grinning face of Red Orc.

'So the fox was caught in my deadfall,' Red Orc said in English.

'Of course, you planned it that way,' Kickaha said.

The Lords were cruel, and this one would want him to die slowly. Moreover, Orc would want him to fully savour the taste of defeat. A Lord never killed a foe swiftly if he could avoid it.

He must keep Red Orc talking as long as he could. If Anana were trying to get close, she would be helped if Red Orc were distracted.

The Lord wanted to talk, to taunt his victim, but he had not relaxed his vigilance. While he lay near Kickaha, he held his beamer ready, and he looked this way and that as nervously as if he were a bird.

'So you've won?' Kickaha said, although he did not believe that Red Orc had won and would not think so until he was dead.

'Over you, yes,' Red Orc said. 'Over the others, not yet. But I will.'

'Then Urthona is still out there,' Kickaha said. 'Tell me, who set up this trap? You or Urthona?'

Red Orc lost his smile. He said, 'I'm not sure. The trap may be so subtle that I was led into thinking that I set it. And then, again, perhaps I did. What does it matter? We were all led here, for one reason or another, to this final battleground. It has been a good battle, because we are not fighting through our underlings, the *leblabbiy*. We are fighting directly, as we should. You are the only Earthling in this battle, and I'm convinced that you may be half-Lord. You certainly do have some family resemblances to us. I could be your father. Or Urthona. Or Uriel. Or even that dark one, Jadawin. After all, he had the genes for red hair.'

Red Orc paused and smiled, then said, 'And it's possible that Anana could be your mother, too. In which case, you might be all-Lord. That would explain your amazing abilities and your successes.'

A thick arm of smoke came down over Kickaha's face and set him coughing again. Red Orc looked alarmed and he backed away a little, turning his back to Kickaha, who was recovering from another coughing fit. Something had happened to his legs. Suddenly, they no longer felt the heat. It was as if dirt had been piled on them.

Kickaha said, 'I don't know what you're getting at, Orc, but Anana could not possibly be my mother. Anyway, I know who my parents are. They were Indiana farmers who come from old American stock, including the oldest, and also from Scotch, Norwegian, German, and Irish immigrants. I was born in the very small rural village of North Terre Haute, and there is no mystery. . . .'

He stopped, because there had been a mystery. His parents had moved from Kentucky to Indiana before he was born, and, suddenly, he remembered the mysterious Uncle Robert who had visited their farm from time to time when he was very young. And then there was the trouble with his birth certificate when he had volunteered for the Army cavalry. And when he had returned to Indiana after the war, he had been left ten thousand dollars from an unknown benefactor. It was to put him through college and there had been a vague promise of more to come.

'There is no mystery?' Red Orc said. 'I know far more about you than you would dream possible. When I found out that your natal name was Paul Janus Finnegan, I remembered something, and I checked it out. And so . . .'

Kickaha began coughing again. Orc quit talking. A second later, a shape appeared through the smoke above him, coming from the other side of the tree where he had thought nothing could be living. It dived through the cloud and sprawled on top of Red Orc, knocking him on his back and tearing the beamer from his hands.

Orc yelled with the surprise and shock and tried to roll after the beamer but the attacker, in a huffled voice, said, 'Hold it! Or I cut you in half!'

Kickaha bent his head as far to one side and as far back as he could. The voice he knew, of course, but he still could not believe it. Then he realized that Anana had piled dirt on them or covered them up with something.

But what had kept her from coughing and giving herself away?

She turned towards him then, though still keeping the beamer turned on Red Orc. A cloth was tied around her nose and mouth. It was wet with some liquid which he suspected was urine. Anana had always been adaptable, making do with whatever was handy.

She gestured at Orc to move away from his beamer. He scooted away backwards on his hands and buttocks, eyeing her malevolently.

Anana stepped forward, tossed her beamer away with one hand as she picked up Orc's with the other. Then, aiming the weapon at him with one hand, she slipped the cloth from her face to around her neck. She smiled slightly and said, 'Thanks for your beamer, Uncle. Mine was discharged.'

Orc looked shocked.

Anana crouched down and said, 'All right, Uncle. Get that tree off him. And quick!'

Orc said, 'I can't lift that! Even if I broke my back doing it, I couldn't lift it!'

'Try,' she said.

His face set stubbornly. 'Why should I bother? You'll kill me, anyway. Do it now.'

'I'll burn your legs and scorch your eyes out,' she said, 'and leave you here legless and blind if you don't get him from under that tree.'

'Come on, Anana,' Kickaha said. 'I know you want to make him suffer, but not at my expense. Cut the branches off me with the beamer so he won't have so much weight to lift. Don't play around. There are two others out there. you know.'

Anana moved away from the smoke and said, 'Stand to one side, Uncle!' She made three passes with the ray from the beamer. The huge branch on his chest was cut in two places; he could not see what she had done to the branch on his legs. Orc had no difficulty removing the trunk and dragging him out of the smoke. He lifted him in his arms and carried him into the woods, where the grass was sparser and shorter.

He let Kickaha down very gently and then put his hands behind his neck at her orders.

'The stranger is out on the boulder,' she said. 'He got up and staggered away just after I got his beamer. He ran there to get away from me and the fire. I didn't kill him; maybe I should have. But I was curious about him and thought I could question him later.'

That curiosity had made more than one Lord lose the upper hand, Kickaha thought. But he did not comment, since the deed was done and, besides, he understood the curiosity. He had enough of it to sympathize.

'Do you know where Urthona is?' he said, wheezing and feeling a pain in his chest as if a cancer had grown there within the last few seconds. His legs were numb but life was returning in them. And with the life, pain.

'I'm not going to be much good, Anana.' he said. 'I'm hurting pretty badly inside. I'll do what I can to help, but the rest is up to you.'

Anana said, 'I don't know where Urthona is. Except he's out there. I'm sure he was the one who set the wolf on fire. And set this up for us. Even the great Red Orc, Lord of the Two Earths, was lured into this.'

'I knew it was a trap,' Orc said. 'I came into it, anyway. I thought that surely I . . . I . . .'

'Yes, Uncle, if I were you I wouldn't brag,' she said. 'The only question the big question anyway is how we get away from him.'

'The Horn,' Kickaha said. He sat up with great effort, despite the clenching of a dragon's claw inside his chest.

Smoke drifted under the trees and made him cough again. The pain intensified.

Anana said, 'Oh!' She looked distressed. 'I forgot about it.'

'We'll have to get it. It must be under the tree back there,' he said. 'And we'll open the gate in the boulder. If worse comes to worse, we'll go through it.'

'But the second room past it is trapped!' she said. 'I told you I'd need a deactivator to get through it.'

'We can come out later,' he said. 'Urthona can't follow us and he won't hang around because he'll think we definitely escaped into another universe.'

He stopped talking because the effort pained him so much.

Red Orc, at Anana's orders, helped him up. He did it so roughly that a low cry was forced from Kickaha. Anana, glaring, said, 'Uncle, you be gentle, or I'll kill you right now!'

'If you do,' Orc said, 'you'll have to carry him yourself. And what kind of position will that put you into?'

Anana looked as if she were going to shoot him anyway. Before Kickaha could say anything, he saw the muzzle end of the beamer fall onto the ground. Anana was left with half a weapon in her hand.

A voice called out from the trees behind them. 'You will do as I tell you now! Walk to that boulder and wait there for further orders!'

Why should he want us to do that? Kickaha thought. *Does he know about the trap inside the gate, know that we'll be stuck there if he doesn't go away as I'd planned? Is he hoping we'll decide to run the trap and so get ourselves killed? He will wait outside the boulder while we agonize inside, and he'll get his sadistic amusement thinking about our dilemma.*

Clearly, Urthona thought he had them in his power, and clearly he did. But he was not going to expose himself or get closer.

That's the way to manage it, Kickaha thought. Be cagy, be foxy, never take anything for granted. That was how he

had survived through so much. Survive? It looked as if his days were about ended.

'Walk to the boulder!' Urthona shouted. 'At once! Or I burn you a little!'

Anana went to Kickaha's other side and helped Orc move him. Every step flicked pain through Kickaha, but he shut his mouth and turned his groans into silence. The smoke still spread over the air and made him cough again and caused even deeper pain.

Then they passed the tree where the Horn was sticking out from a partially burned branch.

'Has Urthona come out from the trees yet?' he asked.

Anana looked around slowly, then said, 'No more than a step or two.'

'I'm going to stumble. Let me fall.'

'It'll hurt you,' she said.

'So what? Let me go! Now!'

'Gladly!' Orc said and released him. Anana was not so fast, and she tried to support his full weight for a second. They went down together, she taking most of the impact. Nevertheless, the fall seemed to end on sharpened stakes in his chest, and he almost fainted.

There was a shout from Urthona. Red Orc froze and slowly raised his hands above his head. Kickaha tried to get up and crawl to the Horn, but Anana was there before him.

'Blow on it now!' he said.

'Why?' Red Orc and Anana said in unison.

'Just do what I say! I'll tell you later! If there is a later!'

She lifted the mouthpiece to her lips and loudly blew the sequence of seven notes that made the skeleton key to turn the lock of any gate of the Lords within range of its vibrations.

There was a shout from Urthona, who had begun running towards them when they had fallen. But as the first note blared out, and he saw what Anana held in her mouth, he screamed.

Kickaha expected him to shoot. Instead, Urthona whirled and, still yelling, ran away towards the woods.

Red Orc said, 'What is happening?'

The last of the golden notes faded away.

Urthona stopped running and threw his beamer down on the ground and jumped up and down.

The immediate area around them remained the same. There was the clearing with its burned grasses, the boulder on top of which the darkly clothed stranger sat, the fallen tree, and the trees on the edge of the clearing.

But the sky had become an angry red without a sun.

The land beyond the edge of the clearing had become high hills covered with a rusty grass and queer-looking bushes with green and red striped swastika-shaped leaves. There were trees on the hills beyond the nearest ones; these were tall and round and had zebra stripes of black, white, and red. They swayed as if they were at the bottom of a sea responding to a current.

Urthona's jumping up and down had resulted in his attaining heights of at least six feet. Now he picked up his beamer and ran in great bounds towards them. He seemed in perfect control of himself.

Not so with Red Orc, who started to whirl towards them, his mouth open to ask what had happened. The motion carried him on around and toppled him over. But he did not fall heavily.

'Stay down,' Kickaha said to Anana. 'I don't know where we are, but the gravity's less then Earth's.'

Urthona stopped before them. His face was almost as red as the sky. His green eyes were wild.

'The Horn of Shambarimen' he screamed. 'I wondered what you had in that case! If I had known! If I had known!'

'Then you would have stayed outside the rim of the giant gate you set around the clearing,' Kickaha said. 'Tell me, Urthona, why did you step inside it? Why did you drive us towards the boulder, when we were already inside the gate?'

'How did you know?' Urthona screamed. 'How could you know?'

'I didn't really *know,*' Kickaha said. 'I saw the slight ridge of earth at several places on the edge of the clearing before we came on in. It didn't mean much, although I was suspicious. I'm suspicious of everything that I can't explain at once.

'Then you hung back, and that in itself wasn't too suspicious, because you wouldn't want to get too close until you were certain we had no hidden weapons. But you wanted to do more than just get us inside this giant gate and then spring it on us. You wanted to drive us into our own gate, in the boulder, where we'd be trapped. You wanted us to hide inside there and think we'd fooled you and then come out after a while, only to find ourselves in this world.

'But you didn't know that Anana had no activator and you didn't know that we had the Horn. There was no reason why you would think of it even if you saw the instrument case, because it must be thousands of years since you last saw it. And you didn't know Jadawin had it, or you would have connected that with the instrument case, since I am Jadawin's friend.

'So I got Anana to blow the Horn even if she didn't know why she was doing it. I didn't want to go into your world, but if I could take you with me, I'd do it.'

Anana got up slowly and carefully and said, 'The Shifting World! Urthona's world!'

In the east, or what was the east in the world they'd just left, a massive red body appeared over the hills. It rose swiftly and revealed itself as a body about four times the size of the Earth's moon. It was not round but oblong with several blobby tentacles extending out from it. Kickaha thought that it was changing shape slightly.

He felt the earth under him tilting. His head was getting lower than his feet. And the edge of the high hills in the distance was sagging.

Kickaha sat up. The pains seemed to be slightly attenuated. Perhaps it was because the pull of gravity was so much reduced. He said, 'This is a one-way gate, of course, Urthona?'

'Of course,' Urthona said. 'Otherwise I would have taken the Horn and reopened the gate.'

'And where is the nearest gate out of this world?'

'There's no harm in telling you,' Urthona said. 'Especially since you won't know any more than you do now when I tell you. The only gate out is in my palace, which is somewhere on the surface of this mass. Or perhaps on that,' he added, pointing at the reddish metamormophosing body in the sky. 'This planet splits up and changes shape and recombines and splits off again. The only analogy I can think of is a lavalite. This is a lavalite world.'

Red Orc went into action then. His leap was prodigious and he almost went over Urthona's head. But he rammed into him and both went cartwheeling. The beamer, knocked out of Urthona's hands by the impact, flew off to one side. Anana dived after it, got it, and landed so awkwardly and heavily that Kickaha feared for her. She rose somewhat shakily but grinning. Urthona walked back to them; Red Orc crawled.

'Now, Uncles,' she said, 'I could shoot you and perhaps I should. But I need someone to carry Kickaha, so you two will do it. You should be thankful that the lesser gravity will make the task easier. And I need you, Urthona, because you know something of this world. You should, since you designed it and made it. You two will make a stretcher for Kickaha, and then we'll start out.'

'Start out where?' growled Urthona. 'There's no place to go to. Nothing is fixed here. Can't you understand that?'

'If we have to search every inch of this world, we'll do it,' she said. 'Now get to work!'

'Just one moment,' Kickaha said. 'What did you do with Wolff and Chryseis?'

'I gated them through to this world. They are somewhere on its surface. Or on that mass. Or perhaps another mass we haven't seen yet. I thought that it would be the worst thing I could do to them. And, of course, they do have some chance of finding my palace. Although . . .'

'Although even if they do, they'll run into some traps?' Kickaha said.

'There are other things on this world . . .'

'Big predators? Hostile human beings?'

Urthona nodded and said, 'Yes. We'll need the beamer. I hope its charge lasts. And . . .'

Kickaha said, 'Don't leave us in suspense.'

'I hope that we don't take too long finding my palace. If you're not a native, you're driven crazy by this world!'

THE STAINLESS STEEL RAT

Harry Harrison

This book introduces Slippery Jim di Griz, cosmic criminal and the smoothest, sneakiest con-man in the known Universe. He can take any bank in the Galaxy, con a captain out of his ship, start a war or stop one – whichever pays the most.
So when the law finally catches up with the Stainless Steel Rat, there is only one thing to do – make him a cop. And turn him loose on a villainous lady who is building herself a battleship.
44377

SCIENCE FICTION 75p

THE STAINLESS STEEL RAT SAVES THE WORLD

Harry Harrison

Someone was tampering with time, altering the past to eliminate the present, fading people out of existence into a timeless limbo. One of the victims was Angelina, the lovely, lethal wife of James Bolivar di Griz – better known as *The Stainless Steel Rat*. His determination to rescue his wife throws him dozens of centuries in both directions including an ancient nation called the United States of America. But then he didn't have much choice; to save Angelina he had to save the world.
44369

SCIENCE FICTION 75p

ILLUMINATUS!

Robert Shea and Robert Anton Wilson

'Nothing is true. Everything is permissible'. – Hassan i Sabbah, founder (1090 A.D.,

Have YOU ever wondered:

WHO IS the MAN in ZURICH that some SWEAR is LEE HARVEY OSWALD?

IF there's an ESOTERIC ALLEGORY concealed n the APPARENTLY INNOCENT legend of Snow White and he Seven Dwarfs?

WHY scholarly anthropologists TURN PALE with terror at the very MENTION of the FORBIDDEN name YOG-SOTHOTH?

Find out in the original and genuine trilogy of CONSPIRACIES battling for world con rol—

ILLUMINATUS!

Volume I THE EYE IN THE PYRAMID
Volume II THE GOLDEN APPLE
Volume III LEVIATHAN

'A cross betwe n a literary acid trip and a political tour de farce' –PLAYBOY